THIEF

B. LOVE

INTRODUCTION

Hey y'all!

Thanks so much for starting this journey with Luca & Riana. Their story was inspired by one line in a song – *hide your heart or keep it from me, thief.* After hearing that, my mind began to race. Three other songs set the tone of this story. Pay very close attention to the song lyrics, as they tell a story of their own.

Write for you soon,

THIEF:

A person who steals another person's property, especially by stealth (cautious action or movement. Slyness. Secrecy) and without using force or violence.

"*D*o you want me to get him for you?"

Riana's jaw clenched. She swallowed hard as her eyes watered. Lowering them, she looked up at David and shook her head softly.

That was Luca's way – handling her away from the eyes and ears of everyone around. At first, Riana thought it was because he wanted her all to himself. Now, she knew the truth; it was because she wasn't the only woman he was entertaining.

Well, she'd always known the truth, but love had her blind. Blind, deaf, dumb, and mute.

No more.

Tonight, her eyes were open, her ears were working, and she was finally using the common sense God gave her.

"No. Just let me through."

David's shoulder's slumped. His expression saddened as he looked her over. Avoiding his eyes, Riana clutched her empty stomach, wondering why it felt as if something was about to erupt. She hadn't eaten anything for the past three days. When she should have felt most weak, Riana felt a strength that had never encompassed her before. With a slow nod, David pulled the rope back and allowed Riana to step into the VIP section that housed Luca, his lady of the night, and the rest of his crew.

Slow, heavy steps led her over to him. The music in the club was blasting, but it was nowhere near as loud as the beating of Riana's heart. Hands grabbed at Riana as she walked that dreaded path to Luca, but she paid them no mind. Her mind was too focused on what Luca's hands were doing on another woman to worry about the ones that were reaching for her.

His woman noticed Riana first. *Her* smile fell as she tilted her head and whispered something into Luca's ear. His eyes closed, and he made no effort to look at Riana until he felt her standing directly over him.

"Can we help you?" *she* asked, wrapping both arms around Luca's right arm.

Completely ignoring *her*, Riana waited for Luca to show her at least a tinge of respect. Surely he wasn't cold enough to disrespect her with another woman right in front of her. Inhaling deeply, Riana pushed her curly hair out of her face. She'd spent hours under the shower stream after her appointment and had no plans of leaving her home – until her cousin sent her a picture of Luca hugged up with another woman.

"What are you doing, Luca?"

Riana's voice was as low and soft as it could be without Luca not being able to hear her. It was best this way. If she yelled, she'd swing.

At them both.

Luca opened his eyes. He looked her over before shaking his head and removing his arm from *her* grip. Standing, Luca grabbed Riana's arm gently and tried to lead her away from the staring eyes, but she jerked herself away from him. There was no hiding his half ass apology when he was so blatant with the disrespect.

"I'll explain in private, Santee."

"No. Explain here. Now."

Luca's head tilted, eyes glancing back at *her* briefly.

"Fine."

"Luca," David called, stepping directly behind Riana. Seemed he cared more about her heart and her feelings than her own man did. Riana's brother, Cameron, had a closer connection to his twin sister, Candace, naturally. Although the siblings were close, Riana sometimes felt left out because of their twin bond. But there was no lack. David's friendship that started when Riana was five had filled any voids being the third wheel to her older siblings left. "Clear the space out or take Ari home."

"No," Riana gritted, turning swiftly to face David. "You always do this, David. You always take his side."

"I'm not taking his side, Ari. I'm looking out for you. This is not something you need to do in public."

It felt easy to lash out on David or anyone else because of her anger towards Luca, but what he'd said was true.

David always looked out for her. And that scared her. If he wanted them to talk privately, he obviously knew something about Luca and *her* that she didn't. Pinching the bridge of her nose, Riana took in a few deep breaths.

Looking in Luca's direction but not his eyes, Riana told him, "Walk me to my car."

"Don't take long, baby," *she* requested, causing Riana to chuckle.

Had David not grabbed her arm, Riana would have given *her* what she was begging for.

"Keep disrespecting me, bitch," Riana warned.

Luca wrapping his arm around Riana wiped the smile from *her* face. "You don't run me. I'll be back when I be back. And when I come back, you better act like you got some sense."

As soon as they were out of the VIP section, Riana pulled Luca's arm down. Crossing hers over her chest, she walked to her car as quickly as she could. She stood out just as much as she did when she walked into the club. All of the women inside were dressed to impress while she had on pajama shorts, a tank top, Nike socks, and slides.

The whole time they walked to her car, Riana's mind tried to convince her that... maybe she didn't want to know the truth. Because there was something in the pit of her telling her that the truth would hurt. Bad as hell. And end what they had. And although Luca had a problem with fidelity, he wasn't a bad guy. He just... wanted what he wanted and didn't accept anything that went against it.

Brushing those thoughts away, Riana decided to stand

firm. They'd been messing around on and off for the past year, and Luca had yet to make things official between them or make her place in his life known to the women that consistently chased him.

Leaning against her car, Riana stared at Luca as he looked everywhere but at her. Normally, he demanded eye contact. His lack of it scared Riana more.

"Just say it, Luca," Riana pleaded, lowering her head and twiddling her thumbs.

"I can't do this with you no more, Santee." Her head lifted. Eyes blinked rapidly. Mouth opened slightly. "It's... ain't no peace here." Luca motioned between the both of them. "When we get together, I get stressed the hell out, and my moves in the streets stress me out enough. I'm not trying to have issues where I lay my head too."

A million things ran through Riana's mind in reply. She could have said that they only had issues because of his lack of commitment and faithfulness. Because he allowed women to disrespect their bond. Because he could some-times act as if he didn't give a fuck about Riana if what she wanted or needed went against his own desires. But instead of saying any of that, Riana nodded as she felt the tears puddle up in her eyes.

"Why'd you have to do this today?" Swiping her tears away, Riana looked to the left of Luca. "I needed you," she mumbled, choking back heavier flowing tears. "I." Swallowing hard, Riana returned her eyes to his. "Need you." Luca's head shook as he took a step away from her. "You can do what you have to do with her, but I... just... need you for the night. I just need you to hold me until I fall asleep, and when I wake up, we can be over."

"Riana..."

"You promised!" Luca grabbed her wrist as soon as her hand shoved his chest. "You said a heart for a heart! I gave you mine, but I've never had yours. Have I?"

Her sadness was beginning to be replaced with anger, causing her to swing at Luca's face with her free hand. Grabbing her wrist, Luca pulled both of her arms behind her and pressed her body into the car. Resting his forehead on hers, Luca exhaled deeply, and as Riana inhaled his exhale, his calmness entered her. He held her there until her breathing slowed down.

"You're the only woman that's ever had access to my heart. I promise you that. But I don't want to settle down right now, Riana, and you deserve better than that." Luca kissed her lips softly. "Than this." He brushed her nose with his gently. "Than me." Releasing her wrists, Luca took Riana's face into his palms by her cheeks, forcing her to look into his eyes. "I'm a motherfucker, that I know. I can't keep hurting you, Riana. Let me go, pooh."

Her eyebrows wrinkled as her eyes squeezed shut. Clawing at his hands, Riana tried to push them from her face, but Luca held on.

"Riana, look at me."

"Just let me go, Luca. You want me to let you go, you're free of me."

A few seconds passed before Luca released her. He'd cut her so deep it was hard to breathe. To stand. Her body grew weak. Sliding down against the car, Riana covered her face, finally allowing her tears to fall freely. Unsure of how much time had passed, Riana weakened even more when she felt arms wrap around her.

There was no need for her to look and see who it was. Those arms enclosed around her and comforted her many nights over the years.

"I'm so sorry," David whispered, lifting Riana to her feet. "I tried to get him not to go out tonight, Ari, but this was his way of dealing with it. I told him that y'all needed to heal together but this was easier for him."

Riana remained silent as she held onto David. Her tears continued to stream down her cheeks. And they weren't just over Luca. They were over the life that was no longer inside of her too.

If Luca wanted to leave, she'd let him, but there was no mistaking it – he'd taken her heart with him too.

UNTITLED

"The thief comes only to steal and kill and destroy."

CHAPTER 1

Riana
(R-E-On-Uh)
Seven Years Later

THIS WAS the third time Riana had switched lanes, and the midnight blue truck did the same. Whoever the driver was, they thought they were slick. They thought Riana wouldn't notice they were trailing her because they let one or two cars stay between them. But she'd been in the streets far too long to ever not be aware of what was happening in her surroundings – even when those surroundings included multiple moving cars.

Clamping down on her gum, Riana let out an irritated sigh as she switched the music from Johnathon Nelson to Kevin Gates. Pinching the bridge of her nose, Riana made one more lane switch just to be sure she was being followed, and as soon as the blue truck moved she chuckled. Pulling her pistol from the center console, Riana rolled her eyes as her speed escalated.

She hadn't even been in Memphis for a good hour and she was already having issues. That didn't surprise her. Those issues were the very reason she left home. Her way of moving and finessing men had made her a target that quite a few people were aiming at.

The escalation of her speed caused the truck to have to do the same. She waited until the truck got directly behind her to slam on her brakes. Swerving, the truck came to a rough stop, trying its hardest to avoid crashing into concrete. Parking in the middle of the street, Riana snatched her bulletproof vest from the back seat. Her eyes remained on the car as she put it on, waiting to see who was about to get out.

At the sight of Amigo getting out of the passenger seat, Riana beat her pistol against the steering wheel with little force. She pushed the door of her car open hard, jumping out quickly. Anger had her aiming the pistol at Amigo even though he was no threat.

"Dammit, Amigo. Are you stupid? I could have killed you."

Hands up in surrender, Amigo took slow steps towards her. "My fault, Ari. I don't have your new number so I couldn't call you to get your attention. Pops wants to talk to you."

Amigo handed Riana his phone as she began to chew her gum again.

"Don't you ever in your life have someone following me unless you want them to come back to you riddled with bullets," Riana greeted, turning her back to Amigo.

The sound of Herbert's low chuckle relaxed Riana. A little.

"I'm about to move your car," Amigo offered, to which Riana nodded.

"You know you can't enter my city and I not find out, beauty. I haven't heard from you in a year. Is it your grandmother's birthday again?"

"Yes. It's today actually. I'm headed her way now."

"I won't hold you long then. Can you come and see me when your family time is over?"

Putting her pistol at her waist, Riana massaged her temple. She hadn't talked to Herbert in a year like he said, and the last time led to a job she should have turned down. Not all money was good money, and for the kinds of enemies Herbert had, Riana valued her life more than a paycheck.

"That's fine, Herbert. I'll be there at seven."

Riana disconnected the call, smiling at the sight of Amigo's smile. "Riana Santee in the flesh. Tell me you gon' let me take you out tonight, sis. We gotta turn up every time you come back home."

Amigo pulled her into an embrace, and Riana willingly returned it. Most people would have expected Riana to have had a romantic relationship with Amigo because he was Herbert's youngest son and the one closest to her age, but that hadn't been the case. If anything, their bond was that of siblings above anything else.

"I'm not staying long, Amigo. I'm actually heading back out tonight."

"Come on now, I know you hate Memphis, but you gotta stay long enough for me to show you off. Leave in the morning. Please?"

Amigo released her just to give her his best puppy dog eyes. With a roll of her eyes and a soft smile, Riana nodded and appeased him with, "I'll let you know when I slide through tonight, okay?"

"Aight cool."

Amigo opened the door for her and Riana got inside, driving off as if nothing had happened. She checked the time on her phone, hoping her run in with Amigo didn't have her late for her grandmother's party. Today, Mary was turning seventy-five years old. After years of living, she'd accumulated everything she could possibly want. Now, her family granted her wishes on her birthday instead of buying her materialistic things.

With no idea of what her grandmother would ask her for this year, Riana was anxious to see her family and grant her wish. This was probably the only thing that made coming back home worth it – her family. Before she left years ago, her relationship with all of them became strained. Not so much because of anything they'd said or done, but because of how life and love dealt Riana a bad hand. One that took her a while and a hell of a lot of solitude to figure out how to play.

But, she'd figured out how to play, and she'd been a master at it ever since.

UNTITLED

"When someone steals your heart not even the law can help you."
— *Matshona Dhliwayo*

CHAPTER 2

iana

RIANA'S MOTHER, Rittany, tightened her grip on her hand. She'd hardly let anyone have more than ten minutes of Riana's time since she'd returned, and her mother's possessiveness was enough to have Riana considering staying home for just a little while longer.

She had been at her grandmother's house long enough for them to eat and listen to some music, now they were hearing and agreeing to grant Grandma Mary's wishes. It was finally Riana's turn, and she was supposed to go and sit next to Mary, but Rittany wasn't having that.

"You can tell her while she sits here, Ma. I don't want to let my baby go just yet."

Resting her head on her mother's shoulder, Riana found

solace in her love. Her way of living didn't help the tension between her and her family, but it was times like this, times where her mother reminded her that she loved her, that Riana lived for.

"Chile, I swear." Even though Mary's voice was stern, there was a smile on her face. "Okay. Riana, this is my wish for you." Riana lifted her head from her mother's shoulder and gave her grandmother her full attention. Mary's smile fell and so did Riana's heart. "We've been hearing the rumors over the years. You running away from them didn't change anything."

Riana clamped down on her gum as she avoided her grandmother's eyes. Those rumors, about her promiscuity, were nothing compared to the bells her nickname rang in the streets. Hell, thinking she was easy with the pussy was nothing compared to them finding out she used it to lure men into her bed just to kill them.

"My wish for you is that you come back home, put all of that foolishness to the side, settle down, and live a normal life, Ari. Heartache hurts, but that is not an excuse to hurt men the way he hurt you. Passing hurt from one blameless heart to another doesn't heal yours; it only makes it grow harder."

Riana smiled with one side of her mouth. Her grandmother had no idea. She wasn't worried about her heart growing harder – Luca still had it in his possession. There was a part of her, though, that desired a normal life. One that didn't require her to have to look over her shoulder and wonder if karma was coming to break even. When she completed jobs for people like Herbert, it was under the name Femme Fatale, true, but a few people started to catch onto the fact that most men that were seen with Riana came up dead or missing.

It didn't matter how much she denied having anything to do with it or the fact that she was the Femme Fatale, men knew, Riana was to be avoided – no matter how beautiful and seductive she was. Now there were a few reckless players that thought they could enter her life and exit with theirs, but her reputation had become one that was hard to live down in a city as small as Memphis.

If she did return home to live a normal life, she would need Herbert's help to clear her name, and if that was the case, she would more than likely have to do whatever he was about to ask her to do.

"I can't promise you that I will settle down, but I can promise you that I will come home and try to be normal."

Even with Riana agreeing, the sarcasm dripped from her lips as she stood.

"She doesn't mean you're not normal, Ari," Rittany spoke softly, standing behind her. "She just wants you to be happy and at peace."

"What makes you think being happy and at peace means I have to have a man and babies? Why can't I be happy living the way I'm living?"

"Are you?" Mary asked, and everyone in the room hung onto the silence for her answer. "Because if you are, you can come back to Memphis and live however you want to live.

I'm getting old, baby. I've wasted enough years out of your life. I just want you close."

It was clear that Mary didn't mean any harm, and Riana tried not to feel so offended, but any time someone mentioned the way she lived that was her reaction. After taking a few deep breaths, Riana shook her head.

"I'm not happy," she whispered, avoiding her grand-mother's knowing eyes. "And I'm not at peace. But that's not because I don't have a man, Grandma."

"I know, baby," was all she said.

"Fine. I will grant your wish."

Mary, Rittany, and Candace filled the room with cheers as Cameron pulled Riana into a bear hug. There was only a matter of time before a mark was missed and Riana had to pay with her life or freedom. Figuring this was the perfect opportunity to get out of the game while she was still on top, Riana allowed herself to embrace the idea of living a life of normality, and as soon as she did, it felt like a literal weight had been lifted from her shoulders.

"I'm happy you're coming back home," Cameron muttered, squeezing her tighter. "If I need to get at any of these niggas let me know."

Riana smiled as she hugged him back. Cameron had no idea. For the enemies she had, it would take more than his big brother protection if she ever had an issue.

UNTITLED

"Love is so powerful that it can enter through a closed door and steal all of the contents of a precious heart within a moment."
— Debasish Mridha

iana

As soon as Riana entered Herbert's home, a flood of memories entered her. Some were good, others were bad, all of them she wished she could forget. It wasn't her intention to meet a man of Herbert's caliber and fall in love with him, especially since he was twenty years older than her. But in that moment, Herbert gave Riana what she needed. Without her father, her daddy issues had her falling in love with every man that showed her the slightest bit of attention, and she clung to them all as if her heart's life depended on it.

It was after her relationship, or non-relationship, with Luca was over that she met Herbert. He took the place of her father, her provider, protector, and her lover. When the space that used to be occupied by her heart was healed, Riana realized how twisted and toxic their relationship was. There was really no love for her in his heart. Herbert was more interested in showing off the pretty young thang on his arm.

Still, even after Riana called things off, Herbert helped her out and kept her close. It was because of his loyalty that Riana started working for him. As one of the biggest drug suppliers in the South, Herbert needed people on his team that he could trust. He groomed Riana into the cold, heartless, lethal woman she was today, and for years she'd been on his payroll as one of his bodyguards and his hit-woman. Eventually, Herbert started using her in a different way.

He used her to lure his enemies into bed before doing away with them.

Riana worked for him for a few years, but eventually, feeling like his work slave became too much. That's when she left Memphis and started taking on her own jobs. Now, she mostly worked with women who wanted to set their husbands up and couldn't catch them cheating. Every once in a while, she'd take a hit job, but that was only when she was sure it would be a quick in and out. If Herbert was requesting her services, it would be to take a life, and since he'd saved hers, it only seemed fair.

Against her mother's wishes, Riana dated Luca. Rittany knew all too well what it was like dating a man like Luca and she forbad Riana to do so. After Riana continued to see him, Rittany exercised tough love and kicked her out. At first, Riana saw no problem with living with Luca and allowing him to take care of her, but when their relationship ended and she was homeless, she saw immediately the problem with depending on a man.

As if the night of their breakup couldn't get any worse, Riana was robbed and sexually assaulted by a homeless man. Had Herbert not been walking down the street to stop their fighting, Riana had no clue what mental state she'd be in today, if she was even alive.

A life for a life – that had always been their agreement. Herbert saved her life, so she took lives for him.

"Since when do you need details on the mark, beauty? Why is your answer no longer an automatic yes?"

Riana massaged the center of her wrist with her right thumb. It was a habit she'd been unable to shake. Not since that night. It was one of the last places he'd touched her, and it was the only way she'd felt connected to him since. Not that she wanted to be connected to him. No. That would be stupid of her. That would be utterly stupid of her to want such a thing.

"I don't work as a hit-woman full time anymore, Herbert. You know that."

Herbert smiled as he sat up in his seat. "I know that, but I didn't know that included me too."

Mirroring his smile, Riana sat up in her seat. "Who is it and why do you want him dead?"

Interlocking his fingers, Herbert licked his lips and remained silent, piquing Riana's interest. Sitting back, he lifted his legs and crossed his ankles on top of the table.

With his hands locked behind his head, Herbert closed his eyes and pulled in a long breath.

"Luca Kareem."

There was no moment of fear greater than the one right now. Riana's heart literally stopped at the sound of his name. This wasn't the first time someone had mentioned him. In fact, her grandmother had done so hours earlier. But this was the first time she'd heard his name in seven years, and that still hadn't been enough time for it to not affect her.

Riana's hand trembled as she slid it down her face. Standing, she wiped her sweaty palms across her pants as she whispered, "No." She grabbed her purse to leave, and Herbert allowed her to get to the door and touch the door-knob before asking...

"Leaving Memphis turned you soft on me?" Riana released the knob but kept her back to him. "He hurt you. Damaged you seemingly beyond repair. That day and night changed you, and it was all because of him. The baby, the breakup, not having anywhere to live, getting raped. That bum tried to kill you, beauty. All of that was because of Luca. And the fact that he told you the biggest, most hurtful lie of all. He said he loved you, but he treated you like shit. He owes you his life, Riana. Make him pay."

He'd been feeding her the same speech over the years, and Riana couldn't help but wonder if this moment was why. She'd come here, making it clear that she was about to retire, and now, he wanted her to kill the only man she'd ever loved. The only man she'd ever given access to her heart to.

The thief.

Luca had stolen her heart with no remorse. No regard. And Riana wasn't sure she'd ever get it back.

Herbert made his way behind her, and although his touch was tender, she froze when his hands squeezed her shoulders. The feel of his lips on her neck made her shudder.

"I've waited to give him to you. It's time, beauty."

Everyone in the streets and law enforcement knew about the war between Herbert's family and Luca's family. It had gotten so bad that any time a murder or crime was committed to one person in the family, they automatically put the other family at the top of the suspect list. The feud started close to twenty-five years ago when Herbert Jacks' father was rumored to have stolen from Luca's grandfather. Ever since, the back and forth feud has led to countless thefts, fights, and murders.

The last? Herbert's middle son was murdered. Although they couldn't prove it, Herbert was sure it was Luca's father or his brother's doing. Even with Luca's father being long gone, Herbert was dead set on making the Kareem family pay, and now... he wanted to use Luca and Riana to do it.

"I can't, Herbert."

"Why not?" Herbert's voice, though calm, was laced with irritation. She turned to face him, and his face was covered with distress. "He stole your heart. Left with it without your permission. Take back what belongs to you, Riana." As if he was sure she would agree, Herbert turned to return to his seat. "I want his heart. I want his life. You owe me this. When you pay up, I will make it clear to the streets that you are off limits. That the Femme Fatale is out of commission. And if anyone gives you a hard time because they suspect you are her, I will handle them personally. But that's only after you deliver him to me. A life for a life, remember? You will not survive in Memphis without me. There are too many bitter women and family members needing answers for the lives of the men you took. You will be a walking target, whether they can prove you are the Femme Fatale or not."

"Okay!" Riana pulled at her hair gently, growling quietly under her breath. "I'll take care of it."

Herbert smiled softly before it turned into a full laugh. "I knew you would."

UNTITLED

"Streets, ain't no falling in love in the, streets
Hide your heart or keep it from me, thief
Know you got some combinations
Know you know I'm on a mission
Listen here, baby listen." – Mila J

CHAPTER 4

uca

LUCA'S PATIENCE was wearing thin. He'd already stopped taking care of business to meet Aaliyah at the airport, and now she was taking forever to hand Tatiana over. It was clear that Tatiana's weight was wearing her hip out, but Aaliyah's grip on her was not loosening up. She'd noticed the extra guards that were surrounding Luca and that only meant one thing – there was a threat that he was trying to avoid. Understandably, she didn't want their daughter caught up in the mix, but to think Luca wouldn't give his own life for Tatiana's was disrespectful in itself.

"I'm not going to say it again," Luca warned, voice just as calm and nonchalant as it always was, but Aaliyah knew just like everyone else to not take Luca's calm demeanor and tone for weakness. "Give me my daughter, Aaliyah."

Aaliyah looked from Luca to his guards, tightening her grip on Tatiana.

"Can't you just come to South Carolina to spend some time with her, Luca? I don't want her around you when it's clear something is going on."

Not wanting to worry her, Luca neglected to tell Aaliyah that word on the streets was that Herbert had put a price on his head. One that he expected the Femme Fatale to carry out. No one could say for sure who the Femme Fatale was, but there were a few speculations. The one Luca refused to believe was that it was Riana. Riana couldn't kill a spider back in the day, so there was no way in hell she was out here finessing men out of their hearts and wallets before killing them.

He hadn't seen Riana since that night, but he was sure of one thing – Riana Santee was *not* the Femme Fatale everyone was painting her out to be.

"That was not the agreement we made."

"This is why I left, Luca. Your life is way too dangerous. I don't want my baby subjected to this. Let me take her back home."

Luca removed Tatiana from Aaliyah's grip effortlessly, and as soon as he held his newly five-year-old daughter in his arms she turned into mush. Luca's heart was just as soft, feeling her tiny arms wrap around him and hold him tightly. Covering her left ear with his hand, Luca pressed Tatiana's right ear and the side of her face gently into his chest so she wouldn't hear him when he said, "You knew who I was when you gave me that pussy. Said you liked that I was in the streets. Don't act like it's a problem now."

"It's always been a problem, Luca!" Aaliyah's arms flailed. "Why do you think I left when I found out I was pregnant? I didn't even want you to know she existed. If you let anything happen to my baby, I will kill you myself."

Luca let her threat slide, watching as Aaliyah walked away.

"I missed you," Luca confessed, turning and carrying Tatiana out of the airport.

"I missed you too, Daddy. Can you take me to grandma's house?"

Luca chuckled as Tatiana stared at the side of his face. "I just got you, and you trying to get away from me already?"

"You can stay there with me."

That was Luca's plan anyway. He wanted Tatiana at his mother's place while he took care of business because he had a guard there at all times. But he knew Tatiana wanted to see her grandmother because she spoiled her rotten.

"I don't want to share you with your grandma, Tati. You can go over there for a few hours, but when I get finished with work you're coming home with me, okay?"

"Yes, sir. I'm going to ask grandma if we can go to the toy store."

And there it was. Luca placed a kiss to Tatiana's forehead after his chuckle died down. He couldn't blame his mother for spoiling her because he spoiled her too. Only difference was, Luca disciplined her as well, and his mother wouldn't even raise her voice to Tatiana. It was crazy how parents treated grandchildren differently. Luca would have sworn his mother's love language was yelling and screaming as much as he and his brother and sister heard it back in the day, but he couldn't think of one time he'd heard her raise her voice these days.

But Luca was no fool.

His mother was a strong, independent black woman that tolerated disrespect from no one, and that was a lot of the reason why Luca didn't either.

Luca put Tatiana in her seat in the back, and for a moment, all he could do was stare at her. Over the years, so many women had tried to nurture his seeds. None of them were successful except for Aaliyah, and that was only because she left town before Luca found out. He swore he didn't want children, but the second he held Tatiana in his arms that changed. There was nothing he regretted about bringing her into this world, not even the woman he went half on her with.

If anything, he regretted not having children sooner.

Not with Aaliyah, but with Riana.

Riana.

She'd been invading Luca's thoughts a lot lately, but just like always, he said a prayer for her and kept it moving. Luca was fully aware of the fact that he'd burned that bridge years ago, and there was no way she'd put that fire out and let him rebuild his way back into her life.

UNTITLED

"Call me a thief
There's been a robbery
I left with her heart
Tore it apart
Made no apologies"

he Past
Riana

IT WAS SAD TO SAY, but gunshots ringing out was so common that everyone in the pool hall didn't even try to leave. They ducked for cover, and once it was calm, everyone returned to their games and conversations. Including Riana. She was there to meet David, and since he was almost always late, she'd been allowing the bartender to entertain her and keep her company.

At twenty-one, she was taking full advantage of finally being of legal age and able to drink. The pool hall and club a few blocks over had become her escapes. Not that there was a huge issue at home with her mother. Rittany was a great mom, but she often forgot that Riana was an adult and not her three-year-old daughter anymore.

Maybe it was because her father wasn't around and Rittany had to raise her and her siblings alone. Whatever the case, Rittany tried her hardest to keep Riana focused on school and home, and it was because of that that she sought excitement and trouble whenever she had the freedom to roam.

Tonight was no different.

The back door burst open, and as soon as Riana's eyes landed on the visibly shaken up trio of men she smiled.

Trouble.

They made their way to the back of the pool hall, and as soon as they sat down, all three men let out sighs of relief. It didn't take a rocket scientist to figure out they were involved in whatever had just happened, nor did it take a rocket scientist to figure out they were to be avoided. But that didn't stop Riana from standing and trying to find a way to catch their attention.

All three men were cute, so she wouldn't have minded which one approached her. But there was something about the dark chocolate god dressed in all black. Something about his rugged handsome features that called to her more. Setting her eyes on him, Riana decided to go to the bathroom, being sure to walk past him with a genuine smile in the process.

By the time she'd made it to their table, the front door was opening. Six police came in, and everyone at the cutie's table froze.

"Ima run for it," the youngest looking one in the group declared, getting a nod out of the brown skinned cutie with dreads.

"*Fuck that shit,*" the dark chocolate god grumbled with a shake of his head. "*I'm tired as hell.*"

Riana chuckled, hating they'd realized she was listening in on their conversation. Standing directly in front of him, she ordered, "Give me what you have." He looked at her like she was crazy and shook his head. "They're in here looking for men. They won't search me. But that's only if I leave before they see me talking to you. Give it to me."

Riana lowered her purse and opened it as he stared at her. His eyes looked around her to the police as they put men on the wall and searched them.

"Give it to her, bro," dread head agreed.

With a sigh and tilted head, the dark chocolate god wrapped his arm around her and pulled her closer. His hand went into the band of his sweats, removing a gun and pair of leather gloves. Dread head handed him a brown bag, and he put it in her purse as well.

"You didn't have this on while you did whatever you did, right?" Riana checked.

"Nah. We dumped our clothes. I'll meet you at the end of the block when the search is over. If we leave now, we'll look suspect."

Completely ignoring the fact that she was supposed to be meeting David, Riana said, "K cool. I'll be in a white Hyundai Elantra."

As she tried to walk away, he grabbed her wrist again. "You steal my shit or give it to them, I'll kill you."

Riana removed her arm from his grip with a slow nod. She returned to the bar and paid her tab before taking steps toward the exit as quietly as she could without drawing attention to herself. Once out of the pool hall, she hopped into her car and drove to the gas station. It felt like forever waiting for the chocolate god to show up, but as soon as she saw him her heart smiled.

He got into the passenger seat of her car, pushing the seat back as if he'd been in it multiple times before. Riana was in no rush to hand him what belonged to him, and he didn't seem to be in a rush to receive it either. She'd parked in the back of the gas station, hidden from the lights, and as he looked her over, she was glad the lights in her car were off too.

Trouble was what she was after, but there was something about the way he looked at her that told Riana she was getting more than what she asked for.

"Why you do that?" he asked, running his hand over the waves in his head.

Riana shrugged, unsure of why she'd risked her freedom for a complete stranger.

"I don't know. Just... wanted to help you."

He nodded as he pulled his phone out. "You know who I am?" Riana shook her head. After checking the time, he put his phone back in his pocket. "I'm Luca. And you are?"

Luca extended his hand for her to shake.

"Riana." She placed her hand inside of his. "Santee."

He smiled, and the bright, whiteness of his teeth in contrast to the darkness of his skin had Riana clamping her legs shut. Not that that dried the wetness that was puddling between her thighs.

"Who are you? You gotta be somebody with a name like that."

With a soft blush, Riana looked away. "I ain't nobody."

Luca's hand went to her chin, pulling her eyes back to him. "Don't say that type of shit. You somebody to me."

Riana chuckled as he released her chin. "Yea, because I saved you from catching a charge."

Luca nodded in agreement. "That's exactly why. You showed me more loyalty than some of the people that share the same blood as me and you don't even know me. For that, anything you need, I got you. That type of loyalty to a nigga like me will have you meaning everything to me."

Her phone began to ring in the cup holder, and the sight of David's picture on it had Luca grabbing it.

"How you know David?" he asked, finger hovering over the accept button.

"That's my best friend."

Luca's expression switched from confusion to realization. "You're Ari?"

Riana nodded as she mumbled, "Yea," taking her phone from him. "Hello?"

"Where you at?" David checked.

"At the gas station up the street. Here I come."

Riana disconnected the call, started her car, and headed back to the pool hall. The entire time she drove the small distance Luca's eyes never left the side of her face. Every few seconds she'd laugh, thinking he still couldn't believe what she'd done for him. Hell, she couldn't believe it herself.

She pulled up, and before she could open her door Luca was telling her, "Stay."

Unable to smile at his gentlemanly gesture of opening her door, Riana's attention went to David as he said, "She's off limits to you, Luca." Ignoring him with a smile, Luca opened Riana's door. He took her hand into his and helped her step out. "You hear me?"

"Are you off limits to me, Santee?"

Santee.

That was the first time anyone had ever called her by her last name, and Riana hated to admit it, but she liked it.

"Don't matter what she says, Luca. I said she's off limits."

"Why?"

"Because she's like my sister and you're a close friend. She's a good girl, and I want her to stay that way. Leave her alone."

Luca didn't acknowledge David's statement either way. He grabbed his things out of Riana's car.

"Thank you," he spoke sincerely before placing a kiss to the center of her forehead and walking away.

"What was that about?"

Riana was unable to answer David right away as she watched Luca walk away. It wasn't until he was out of her sight that she was able to say, "Nothing."

"I'm serious, Ari. Luca is cool as hell, but he's a dog. Don't mess with him."

Riana nodded as she turned to close the door. When she noticed the thick stack of cash on the seat she started to go *after Luca to give it to him, but there was no way he could have mistakenly left that behind because the bag was sealed shut. He'd intentionally left that. For her. Grabbing the phone that was next to it, Riana put the money in her purse and headed inside of the pool hall with David.*

All night, her thoughts were clouded with Luca. His walk. His voice. His demeanor. His looks. The way he looked at her.

It didn't matter how much she told herself to listen to David and leave him alone... if she ever had the chance... there was no doubt in Riana's mind that she'd allow him to pursue her.

Since the phone was locked, Riana was unable to go through it. But she didn't have to. By the time she'd made it home and showered it was getting a call. Since it wasn't her phone she ignored the call, but a text came through.

It's Me, *was all it said, but Riana was fully aware of who* me *was.*

He called back, and Riana wasted no time answering.
"Hello?"

"What's your address? I'm about to come and scoop you up. Or would you rather meet me somewhere?"

A wide smile covered Riana's face at the sound of Luca's voice. David's warnings be damned. They weren't strong enough to keep her from almost purring, "You can come and get me."

UNTITLED

"I've been living in the darkness
Shadows in my apartment, heartless
Taking love just to spill it on parchment
Next page and I'm out again"

CHAPTER 6

 iana

RIANA'S HAND slid across the silk garment, awakening her senses immediately. Being a woman who loved pampering herself and splurging, Riana was used to taking spa and shopping trips at least twice a week, but now that she'd agreed to living a normal life, she'd started to cut back on blowing her money so recklessly. Instead of purchasing anything today, she allowed herself to window shop, and window shopping led to going inside and feeling the clothes. Now, she was talking herself out of trying the shirt on.

"What do you think about this, Tati? Do you think your aunty would like this for her birthday?"

The sound of the woman's voice was familiar, but Riana couldn't place where she knew her from. Deciding not to draw attention to herself, she chose not to turn around and look at the woman's face. Unable to resist, Riana removed the shirt from the rack and headed to the dressing room to try it on. The feel of the silk against her skin satisfied a need she'd been craving more and more over the years. A need that no man had been able to fill. Not since Luca. A need to be touched and soothed in a way that she couldn't explain to even receive.

Forcing herself to not need things, sex, or men to satisfy her void, Riana held firm to not buying anything on this trip. When she went to put the shirt back on the rack, she was met by the biggest set of glossy, marble brown eyes she'd ever seen on a human so small. Her ebony black hair was natural, pulled into two high puff balls. A round face with puffy cheeks housed the prettiest features. Riana was convinced, this little girl was an angel.

"You're pretty," she complimented Riana, looking up at her as if she was a giant.

With a smile, Riana lowered herself so that they were eye to eye.

"You're pretty too, doll face. How old are you?"

With a proud smile, she held up her hand and all but yelled, "Five."

"Five?" Riana chuckled as she nodded rapidly. "You're a big girl."

"I sure am." Her fingers slid across Riana's freckles. "I wish I could have pink hair. It's so pretty."

A warm feeling oozed through Riana's heart that she wasn't quite used to. Her fingers went from Riana's cheek to her hair. Riana couldn't think of anything to say as this little human stared almost mesmerized by her – just as mesmerized as Riana was of her.

"Aye, where the fuck is my baby?"

Clutching her heart, Riana's eyes snapped shut at the sound of his voice. There was no denying that voice or the effect it had on her. *Now* she knew where she'd heard the female voice from. It belonged to Luca's mother.

Luca.

He was here.

He couldn't be.

Riana wasn't prepared to see him yet.

"I don't know, Luca. I looked away for just a second to grab my phone and when I looked back up Tati was gone."

Snapping out of her trance, Riana asked her, "What's your name, doll face?"

"Tatiana."

"I think your family is looking for you. Did you wander away?"

She lowered her head slowly, smile fading.

Riana stood. She took Tatiana's hand into hers and slowly walked her around the racks that separated her from her father and grandmother. Her plan was to put Tatiana behind them and walk away, but the second her eyes landed on Luca she froze.

"Grandma, look! I found a real-life fairy. Isn't she pretty?"

Both Lucy and Luca looked back at the sound of her voice. Lucy snatched Tatiana up and into her arms, hugging her tightly, chastising her with a soft voice for walking away. Riana expected Luca to do the same, but he was too busy staring at her to say or do anything.

This seemed like the perfect time to squeeze her way back into his life, but the longer she stared into his eyes the more she felt like that lost, hopeless soul she was the night they broke up years ago. Well, technically, it wasn't a breakup because their relationship wasn't official, but that didn't stop every piece of Riana's heart and soul from breaking over the lack of Luca.

Turning on her heels, Riana headed for the exit, sure her heart would explode into tiny pieces if she was in his presence much longer.

"Riana, wait!"

"That was Ari?" Lucy checked, causing Riana to walk even faster.

"Santee." Luca's arm wrapped around her waist, and her steps stilled at the mention of her name. Luca was the only person to call her by her last name. Said it sounded bad ass and savage as fuck. Said if they ever got married he'd want to take *her* last name. Said it like she belonged to him and he'd given it to her, because it never sounded the same coming out of anyone else's mouth. "Please don't leave," he requested quietly, pressing his body into the back of hers.

Legs going limp, Riana clung to his arm for strength.

"She's beautiful," Riana admired, choking back tears at

the thought of the baby that was supposed to be theirs to share.

"Thank you for bringing her back. I was about to go on a rampage."

Even though Riana wasn't facing him, she could hear the smile in his voice. Just as clearly as she heard the fear when Tatiana was missing. For someone who never wanted children, he'd created a beautiful child, and obviously loved her terribly so.

"I have to go, L–" She couldn't even force herself to say his name. She couldn't even bear the taste of it. The sweetly bitter stain that coated her tongue just as thick as saliva.

"We need to talk." Luca's right hand went to her waist, and he used it to turn her around to him, but Riana avoided his eyes. "There's a lot that I have to say to you, including an apology, and this is not the time or the place."

The contract she'd signed for Herbert made her want to say yes. Why, Luca was literally putting himself in her web. But the memories, the pain, the scars along the vessels that used to hold her heart... he'd left her rib cage empty, exposed, rotting, full of holes... that dark, shallow space was screaming, begging no.

"Santee." Riana looked at him, but it wasn't for a full second before she was looking away again. "Can I take you to lunch or something tomorrow?" With a slow nod, Riana stepped back and put some space between them. "Is one o'clock okay?" She nodded. "At Interim?" She nodded again. "Cool." Riana turned to leave, stopping when he called her name. "Tati was right; you are pretty. You're beautiful."

Grinding her teeth, Riana continued out of the store without muttering a word.

UNTITLED

"I've been living in the night life
Lips hit you like a drive by, frost bite
Ice cold, I mean they cut you like a sharp knife
Next page and I'm out again"

CHAPTER 7

uca

Luca's leg shook anxiously as he awaited her arrival. This was why she'd been on his mind so much lately. It had to have been God's way of preparing him to see her. But there was no amount of preparation for that moment. Had she not walked away and forced him to speak, Luca probably would've still been standing there staring if she would have let him.

Riana was the only thing Luca regretted in his life. While he in no way expected them to ever get back together again, he was grateful for the opportunity to right the wrongs he'd done towards her. As he waited for her to join him at the restaurant, Luca checked in on his businesses, legal and illegal. With Tatiana living in a completely different state, his businesses were his babies. They were what he lived for. What kept him focused and looking forward to waking up every morning.

He felt her before he saw her. Putting his phone back in his pocket, Luca looked up, smiling immediately at the sight of her walking over to the table.

Luca stood and walked over to what would be her side of the table. He waited until she stood directly in front of him to greet her with, "Hey."

"Hi."

"I'm glad you could come."

Riana nodded as she avoided his eyes. After pulling her seat back, Luca stood behind her as she sat down, unable or not even desiring to stop himself from sniffing her neck and brushing his nose against it in the process.

"You smell so good," he complimented, pushing her chair up to the table.

And she definitely did.

She smelled candy sweet. Almost like cotton candy.

"Thanks."

Luca could tell by her tone and stiff posture that she was ready to go already, so he made his way back to his seat, fully prepared to say what he had to say and let her go. But when he looked her over, rushing was the last thing on his mind. Dressed in all black, Riana looked just as beautiful as she did yesterday.

Honey brown skin wrapped around her tall, slim

frame. Her pink hair sat atop her head in a messy bun. A bang covered her forehead, but thankfully, she had it pushed away and allowed him to see her eyes. Her beautiful eyes. They were slanted and almond shaped. Her dark eyes were illuminated by the light eyeliner she had on.

Luca's eyes scanned the freckles on her nose and high cheeks. He'd spent many nights cuddled up next to her, giving her nose Eskimo kisses that made her giggle and bite down on her bottom lip. His attention went from her septum piercing to her burgundy colored heart shaped lips.

"How have you been, Santee?"

For the first time, Riana looked at him for longer than a second. She shrugged and clutched her wrist. When Luca's eyes lowered to it, Riana pulled her hands under the table.

"Good. You?"

"Same. Seeing you after all this time..."

"Can you just say what you have to say?"

Her irritation caused Luca to smirk. The waitress returned to take Riana's drink order, but she declined. Deciding to end this before she started spazzing for old times' sake, Luca went ahead and did what he'd been wanting to do for years.

"I'm sorry, Riana." Her eyebrows scrunched up and mouth opened partially, but she shut it as she swallowed and looked away from him. "For the way I treated you while we were talking and for how I ended things." Luca reached across the table and used her chin to turn her head back in his direction. "When I ended things."

Riana grabbed his water and took a sip, getting a quiet chuckle out of him before he continued.

"I'm sorry for loving you and giving you reasons to fall in love with me knowing I didn't want to be in a relationship." Her head dropped. "I'm sorry for not being faithful to you while expecting you to be loyal and faithful to me." Her shoulders caved. "I'm sorry for not giving you the honor and respect you deserved." Her head shook. "I'm sorry for pushing you to have an abortion." Her shoulders shuddered. "I'm sorry for not being there for you when you needed me most." She chuckled quietly, brushing a stray tear from her cheek. "I'm sorry for it all, pooh."

When her face was clear of tears, she lifted her head and looked into his eyes.

"I know me apologizing doesn't take away the pain, but at least I'm acknowledging how fucked up I treated you. You didn't deserve that, Riana. Not at all."

"Thank you," she almost whispered, avoiding his eyes again.

If it was anyone else, Luca would have been irritated by the lack of eye contact. With Riana, though, he knew her well enough to know she only avoided a person's eyes when she was feeling vulnerable or in her feelings. Apparently, his apology opened her up a bit too because when the waitress returned with Luca's appetizer she ordered a drink and a plate of crab and corn fritters.

"Why are you apologizing? It's been years. Even if you felt like it was wrong, I chose to put up with what you were doing. Where is this coming from?"

"Tatiana." Luca smiled just at the thought of his daughter. "Her mother was the first woman I dealt with on a consistent basis after you. She was cool with us not being in a relationship because, although she enjoyed the excitement of being with a bad boy, she didn't want to be attached to me and a target because of my lifestyle. We fucked around for a good little minute before she got pregnant. Aaliyah just... up and left.

I wasn't fucked up about it because, unlike you, she was replaceable to me. About six months later, one of my homeboys went to South Carolina for an event and saw her there. Big belly and all. Even though I didn't want kids, I didn't want my child out here and I not be in their life. I confronted her about it, and unlike you, she was too far along to have an abortion. Didn't really want to accept that I was having a kid, but as soon as I held Tatiana in my arms all that shit was over.

I fell in love with her immediately and wanted to do everything I could to give her the best life possible. Having a girl changed the way I handled women. Made me not want to do anything to degrade or devalue them because I'd kill a nigga if he did a fraction of the shit I did to my daughter. It was because of her that I realized how fucked up I'd treated you, and when I did realize that shit, I broke down and cried, Santee."

Luca exhaled a loud breath and took a sip of his water, feeling himself get worked up all over again.

"I wanted to reach out to you sooner and apologize, but I didn't want to disrupt your life like that. I just promised myself that I would do so if we ever crossed paths again."

Silence found them until Riana's appetizer was delivered. She took one bite before asking, "Are you with her mother now?"

"Nah. We're good with co-parenting, but we get on each other's nerves too much to ever try to be in a relationship." They both smiled and chuckled quietly, but Luca was dead serious. "Are you married? I didn't see a ring, but I still need to ask."

Riana's smile widened, lifting her already high cheeks until her eyes almost closed.

"I'm not married. No. You don't care if I'm in a relationship?"

Luca's expression turned serious as he sat back in his seat. "Not at all. If you didn't make vows before God I don't give a fuck what you got going on with a man."

Riana nodded, pushing her plate to the side. "Well, no, I'm not in a relationship either, but..."

"You don't have to say it, Santee. I know we won't ever be together again, and I'm okay with that. But I do want to right the wrongs I did against you. I want to replace the pain I caused you. I know I can't do anything about the baby we..." Luca's chest caved, closing in on his slowly beating heart. "But I want to replace all the bad thoughts and memories you may have of me. That's only if you want me to, though."

He expected it to take a while for Riana to agree, so he was caught completely off guard when she said, "That's fine with me. Just as long as you don't expect much from me."

That seemed fair, seeing as he'd said the same thing to her years ago.

While they waited on their food, they continued to converse and catch up. Luca shared with her what had been going on in his life lately. How he was heavier in the drug game now and had added a few legal businesses under his belt as well. He had a sports bar and lounge. She asked him if he still wanted to go to college, and he told her yes. Riana was the only person he'd ever shared that with, and she was the only person that made him feel like it was possible.

It would be strange, going from drug dealer to lawyer, but that's what Luca wanted to do. One day, maybe after he retired, he'd return to school. But without a woman like Riana at his side to encourage and support him, Luca figured that would always be just a dream.

Their conversation got a little deep when Riana began to fill Luca in on what she'd been doing lately. She told him about her career as a technical writer, and although he'd heard of it before, he didn't really know exactly what they did.

"I create instruction manuals and things like that. Basically, I simplify the complex for companies and consumers."

Luca's face twisted up, causing Riana to laugh. "That sounds..."

"Dry and boring as hell?" They both nodded as she chuckled. "It is."

"How'd you get into that? Why'd you get into that?"

Riana shrugged, avoiding his eyes. "My first year of college was undecided because I didn't know what to do with my life. I had a work study job on the newspaper team, and I enjoyed it. That led to me majoring in professional writing. But, I chose to make technical writing my niche because it balanced the wild lifestyle I was living, and it gave me control over something, you know? It allowed me to simplify and give meaning and answers to something during a time when I had so many questions about myself, my life, and the hand I was dealt."

Luca wasn't sure why he felt like that was the time to ask, but he asked, "Are you the Femme Fatale?" anyway.

Riana smiled softly before taking a sip of her water. "Do you think I'm capable of something like that, Luca?"

He stared into her eyes, unable to find an answer to his question.

"The Riana I knew back in the day wasn't, but people change. I've changed, maybe you changed too."

She nodded as she pushed her seat back, causing Luca to stand. He wasn't expecting their lunch to have such an abrupt end, but she'd agreed to letting him fix his fuck ups, so that was okay with him.

"That's true, but it seems like you've changed for the better."

"I like to believe I have. Let me walk you out."

"No, that's not necessary. Enjoy the rest of your lunch."

Riana pulled her wallet out of her purse, but she put it back after Luca insisted on paying. They exchanged numbers, and Luca watched as she walked away. What he'd said was true – he didn't expect them to ever get back together, but he was most definitely going to make the most of having Riana Santee back in his life. And maybe, just maybe, if God agreed, he'd be able to bless her with a baby. It wouldn't replace the one they'd lost, but it would most definitely feel like a Balm in Gilead.

UNTITLED

"Skin on my skin, what a wonderful sin
Take your breath but you're asking for more"

CHAPTER 8

The Past
Luca

IT WAS *their first official date, and Luca was confident that he knew Riana well enough to make the night perfect for her. She liked seafood and being to herself. As the youngest child, Riana was spoiled. Like most families in the hood, her mother didn't have much when she was a kid, but that didn't stop her from busting her ass to give Riana everything she possibly could. More than that, her mother spoiled her with her love and attention, and Luca was sure that was something he could emulate.*

The first night he picked her up, Rittany wasn't home. The second night she was, and she made it clear she didn't want Riana to have anything to do with him. Riana may not have known who Luca was, but Cameron and Rittany knew who he was in the streets. Luca thought that would pull Riana away from him. So far, she was still rocking with him.

To avoid unnecessary drama, Luca started to tell Riana to meet him at the restaurant, but he put his pride to the side and prepared to listen to anything negative Rittany had to say. Thankfully, her car wasn't outside when Luca pulled into their driveway. He got out of the car and went to get his woman, roses in hand. Cameron opened the door, making it clear he wasn't pleased with his sisters' choice in men.

"She's a grown woman. If she wants to fuck with me that's none of your concern," Luca replied in his naturally calm tone.

"She will always be my concern. Don't get my sister caught up in your shi—"

"Oh my God. Will you go somewhere and stop embarrassing me," Riana almost yelled, pushing past Cameron.

"Didn't mama tell you she didn't want you dealing with this dude, Ari?"

Riana smiled as Luca handed her the flowers.

"You look beautiful, Santee."

"Thank you," Riana cooed, smiling harder when he took her hand into his to lead her to his car.

"Alright, Ari. I'm telling mama."

"So!" she yelled, face scrunching up immediately, but as soon as Luca pulled her into his side her expression softened. "I'm sorry about him."

"It's cool." Luca opened the door for her, buckling her seatbelt once she was seated comfortably. "I know we just started kicking it, but if they get on your nerves about me too much, you can come and stay with me."

Riana stared at him blankly for a few seconds before shaking her head no.

"I appreciate the offer but I'm good. Thanks, Luca."

With a nod, Luca stood upright and closed the door. On the ride to their first destination, Riana was fairly quiet. She was strange. While speaking to and handling everyone else, she was tough and outspoken. With him, she was shy and quiet. Since that night, he hadn't seen the quick-thinking rider, only this innocent, submissive beauty.

They made it to the movie theater, and Luca was glad he'd planned their date the way he had. The first part was an old movie that would allow them to have the theater alone. He was hoping that gave her time to get comfortable being in his presence again. Seemed like it always took her a while to open up and start talking to him when they linked up. This way, she'd have a full two hours to be quiet while the movie was playing.

To his surprise, she held his hand and cuddled up against him the whole time. His phone went off several times in his pocket, but in that moment, Luca's only priority was Riana.

After the movie, they went to the mall. Normally Luca wouldn't dare go shopping with a woman, but he was anxious to see how different colors would look and textures would feel against Riana's skin.

The first dress she tried on was a white, strapless maxi dress. It was cute. Something she could wear for anything.

The second dress she tried on was a black knee length,

form fitting dress that had his dick on hard as she modeled it for him.

The third dress was the one that did it. The one that had Luca lifting himself off the wall and following Riana back into the dressing room, locking the door behind them. It was red – the color he'd decided was his favorite to see her in. The sleeves were long, and it stopped mid-thigh. There was a long v-cut down the middle, exposing the sides of her breasts. It stopped just under her belly button, showing off her diamond studded belly ring.

"Are you here to help me take this off?" Riana asked through her smile.

Luca chuckled as he turned her towards the mirror. "Nah." He pushed her hair over her left shoulder and kissed the right side of her neck. "Leave it on."

Slowly, his fingers slid down her arms. Over her breasts. Down her stomach. It wasn't until she moaned and tilted her head back did he think to ask, "Is it okay if I touch you?"

With lust lowered eyes, Riana moaned, "Do whatever you want to me."

Her willingness to surrender herself to him caused a groan to slip from deep within Luca's throat. On his knees, Luca lifted Riana's dress slightly. After pushing her panties to the side, he noticed she was already dripping and ready for him. Still, Luca used his hand in the center of her back to lower the top part of her body to the bench. He waited until her fingers gripped it to spread the lips of her pussy and lap up all that she'd left for him.

His tongue slid up and down between her folds as Luca

spread her ass cheeks apart. Latching onto her clit, his dick throbbed at the sound of her moan. He sucked until she dripped, quenching a thirst for her that he'd been ignoring ever since he laid eyes on her. Tongue stiffened, Luca pressed it into her opening, gripping her waist the second she locked up and moaned. He alternated between tongue fucking her, sucking her clit, and slurping every drop that dripped between her folds until she came.

On his feet, Luca chuckled at the sight of Riana trembling and trying to compose herself as he removed himself from his boxers. Holding her steady, Luca informed her, "You got one last chance to change your mind, Santee," as he put the head of his dick at her opening.

Riana's nails dug into the bench. "Luca." Her eyes found his. "I want you in the worst way."

Not needing to hear anymore, Luca entered her with one swift stroke. One that had her snatching in a deep breath as she tried to pull away from him. There wasn't a soft or romantic bone in his body, until he met Riana. He'd been racking his brain trying his hardest to come up with ways to wine and dine her.

But sex?

Nah.

That would always be rough. And fast. And hard. And detached.

But as she squirmed against him, Luca couldn't help but ask, "You dan had dick before, right?"

Just to be sure. Because they'd talked about sex before. And she'd said she wasn't a virgin. But her inability to take this dick had him wondering if she'd be able to handle it.

"Yea, but not like this." Luca pulled out, and a devious thought came to his mind. Slowly, he entered her, clenching her by the hips just as tightly as her walls clenched his dick. "Not one this big." He'd have to take his time with her. "Not this good." Train her, teach her.

Luca pulled out, looking down at the slick film of her juices that had started to coat him.

And she'd be teaching him too. Teaching him how to please and take his time with a woman. Train him to see them as more than just a means to nut.

He entered her with only half of his length, just to exit her. She was so wet the popping sound of her pussy bounced against the walls. Stroking just the ridges of her G-Spot, Luca closed his eyes and tried to focus on anything but her heavy breathing and quiet moans. Unable to do so, he pressed all of him inside of her, groaning as she cursed. Filling her with slow, deep strokes, Luca watched as her cream slathered his shaft and trickled down her thigh.

Her warmth. Her grip. Her her.

"Luca," she moaned, arching her back more. She was ready. "Baby." Pushing herself into him, Riana took all of Luca, whimpering as his strokes sped up. "Yesss," she cried, body locking and walls pulsing as she came.

Luca wanted desperately to feel her cum against him, but if he stayed inside he would cum too, and it was too soon. He sat down and lifted her on top of him. Her back arched as he filled her again. The sight of her biting down on her bottom lip, hair frazzled, eyes low... was enough to have him ready to cum on its own.

He guided Riana's movements, unsure of if she had any experience riding or not. In no time, she found her own rhythm. Luca relaxed under her, allowing himself to get lost in her flow. She was probably the most sensual woman he'd ever come in contact with. From the way she placed his hands where she wanted them to go to the way she licked and sucked his fingers as he throbbed inside of her. How she'd make sounds to express her pleasure to the way she looked into his eyes with such need and satisfaction. Even how the sound of his pleasure seemed to intensify hers turned Luca on.

"Are you on birth control, pooh?" Luca muttered, gripping her hip with one hand while he fingered her clit with the other. His legs stretched out as his body jerked underneath her. "Riana." She moaned, squeezing his shoulders as her walls began to close against him again. Holding a palm full of her hair, Luca pulled her head down and forced her to look at him as he called, "Santee."

"Hmm?"

"Are you on birth control?"

"No," she moaned, bucking against him as she came.

Luca beat his head against the wall gently, trying his hardest to hold back his orgasm until hers subsided. He allowed her to wildly ride him until he couldn't take anymore, then he lifted her up as he came himself.

Riana rested against him as they both composed themselves.

Thankfully, she had a package of Kleenex in her purse. It held them over until they made it out of the dressing room to clean up as best as they could in the restroom.

Luca purchased all three dresses and two pairs of shoes before they left. It was his plan to let her shop until she dropped, but after exerting so much energy in the dressing room, Riana wanted to eat and take a nap.

They went to her favorite seafood restaurant for dinner, where they got to know each other a little better. He already knew the big facts about her, like who she came from and what she wanted to do with her life. She wasn't in college, but she worked full-time in her aunt's clothing store. It was more important to her now to work and help take care of her sister's daughter, her niece, than to go to school, but she planned to enroll before she turned twenty-five.

They even talked about the simple things. Like their likes and dislikes. Favorite colors and things to do. Goals and where they wanted to travel. Nothing was off the table, but Luca was ready to call it a night when Riana asked...

"What are your intentions with me?" Luca wiped his mouth as Riana added, "I know I probably should have asked that before we..." She covered her face and giggled in a way that made Luca want to take her to the bathroom so they could do it again. Her hands lowered as she shook her head. "But what exactly do you want from me?"

Luca sat back in his seat, massaging his chin. It wasn't a difficult question, and he knew the answer in his mind, but his heart...

"I don't do commitment, and I fuck around." Luca

paused and gave Riana time to digest what he'd said. "What David said was true, I'm a dog ass nigga, Santee."

Her eyes saddened as she sunk in her seat.

"Then why are we here?"

"Because I like you." Luca reached across the table for her hand. "I don't do this for women. Dates and shit. I'll blow money on them, but that and sex is as far as it used to go. But it's just... some about you, Riana Santee."

She smiled bitterly. Eyes watered before she looked away.

"I don't want to be another woman on your roster. I don't want to be number one if I'm not the only one."

Luca scratched his head as he nodded. His legs spread as his heart raced. Settling down wasn't his desire. Had never been, never would be. Sure, he loved having his pick of women, but more than that, he never wanted to subject them to the pain his mother sustained every time the fathers of her children left.

He was young, and he wanted to be wild and live free. "And I don't want to let you or anyone else tame me."

"Okay." Riana nodded, still avoiding his eyes. She looked at him long enough to say, "You can take me home now," before looking away.

"You haven't eaten."

Her eyes tightened as she gritted, "I don't have an appetite."

Riana stood to leave, and Luca slowly followed behind. He opened the door of his car for her, heart breaking as she continued to avoid his eyes. She remained silent for the entire ride. It wasn't until he walked her to her door that she said, "Thank you, for everything."

She tried to open the door, but he closed it and pressed her against it.

"You gon' cut me off, Santee?"

"What other choice do I have, Luca?"

He thought over her question until she sighed and tried to open the door again. "You can still be mine. Without the titles and expectations. I'll still treat you good, Riana."

"Yea, but you won't be just mine. And I deserve better than that."

"You do, but I would be a fool to let you go."

"I agree." She smiled, and so did he. "All you have to do is do right by me."

Luca's head shook as he decided to stand firm on his choice.

"I can't, pooh."

"I understand." Riana stepped on the tips of her toes and kissed his cheek. "Goodbye, Luca."

He watched her walk into her home, determined to make her his. With Riana Santee at his side, there would be nothing Luca couldn't do.

UNTITLED

"The tip of my finger is tracing your figure
I say good night and walk out the door"

 iana

As Riana stood in front of Luca's door, she considered leaving before he opened it. The fact that he appeared to be a better version of himself, a better version of himself with a daughter, had Riana reconsidering her part in his demise. It was the contract, the contract for a life for a life, that was keeping her feet planted. The contract made clear that Riana was the only person capable of bringing Luca to his demise, and if she didn't, wouldn't, or couldn't, Herbert wanted her life instead.

She'd been brewing and stewing ever since she left his place, knowing this was his plan all along. He never truly cared for her as he promised he did. From the very beginning, Herbert was aware of who Riana was, and he knew what she meant to Luca – even if Luca didn't want to acknowledge it. There would come a day when Riana would be Luca's greatest weakness, and Herbert waited until that day came to capitalize.

It was going to be a cold blow to Luca's ego, losing his life to the only woman he claimed to love, but there was nothing Riana could do to change that now. And a part of her still didn't want to. Yes, Luca could potentially be a good man now, but that still didn't excuse what he'd done to her years ago. The pain she'd sustained because of him. With that thought in mind, Riana inhaled a deep breath, put on her game face, and said a quick prayer as she heard Luca unlock the door.

Not to God. No. She was sure he wouldn't hear her during a time like this. But to herself. That she wouldn't blow this and jeopardize losing her own life because she became putty in his hands all over again. As far as she was concerned, Riana had given enough because of her love for Luca. Her life was something she refused to give.

They'd been talking on the phone and texting for the past week, and it wasn't for a lack of effort on Luca's part to spend time together again. Finally, he'd convinced her to come to his place since she wasn't comfortable going out with him yet. Lunch in the middle of the day was one thing, a date at night was a whole other. Not only was Riana careful about being seen with him before his death, she also didn't want people from her past to look at her crazy for being with him after all they'd gone through.

Not that she gave a damn about what people thought about her.

Then again, maybe she did.

As soon as the door opened fully, and Luca was within sight, all of the pain and bitterness she'd been holding in slowly began to dissolve. The longer he stared at her, the more she... felt. *Felt*. And she hadn't done that with anyone else. Not since him. Her family, her loves, those were the only people over the years who could make her feel. She'd sworn she was heartless and could not be swayed emotionally, but as usual, here was Luca – changing everything she thought she knew about herself.

This was dangerous for her too, and the second Luca took her hand into his and gently pulled her into his home she laughed in nervousness at that truth. Her heart hadn't been this close to her in what felt like forever, and with it being so close, even still in Luca's possession, those vessels around Riana's heart were softening and coming back to life. Those ribs that were closed, cracked, and riddled with holes just like her soul, were slowly starting to heal themselves.

As if they knew it was time to prepare.

Time to prepare for her heart to return again.

But at what cost?

"May I hug you?" Luca asked after closing the door behind her, and Riana wasn't sure if she could handle that. It was already hard having him brush against her to get to the door.

Cupping her hands in the center of her, Riana allowed

her eyes to take in the rugged handsome man that stood before her. He was the same height, but the muscled weight he'd put on over the years made his build look different. It was covered with bitter, dark chocolate toned skin, and Riana was hoping it was still free of tattoos. Perfect skin like that was too flawless of a canvas to be stained by anything.

The low cut fade he rocked accentuated his square shaped face. It was tapered, connected with his stubbly, extended goatee beard combination. Tight, dark under turned eyes lowered and scanned Riana's body as she did the same to him, but her eyes kept returning to his face. To those top and bottom gold grills. And how they combined with his chain and pierced ears to have her pussy throbbing in anticipation of having him there all over again.

Because, it would be justified. It would be what she always did. Sex with Luca would mean nothing besides a ploy to get him to open up to her. That's what she kept repeating as she nodded and allowed him to embrace her, but as soon as his arms engulfed her Riana accepted her fate – there was no way she could do anything with Luca Kareem and not be affected by it personally, no matter how much she told herself returning to his life was for professional reasons only.

UNTITLED

"Call me a thief
There's been a robbery
I left with her heart
Tore it apart
Made no apologies"

iana

HE'D FIXED her favorite meal – Cajun seafood pasta and garlic bread along with a spinach and kale salad. At first, Riana tried her hardest to remain cold and detached, but the more he made the effort to talk and reconnect the less she cared about harboring ill feelings towards him and focused on how good being around him felt in her present.

That changed when "Love and Happiness" by Al Green began to play in the background. As it did in the past, all conversation ceased. Riana smiled, lowering her head to hide it as Luca stood. His hand extended for her to take, and there was no way she could dance with him like back in the day. Being in his arms in that way would make this moment too real. Too poignant. Too intimate.

"This was a mistake," she muttered, standing and snatching her purse to leave, but Luca grabbed her by her wrist and pulled her into his chest.

"Why is it a mistake, Santee?" Luca pushed her bang to the side so he could look fully into her eyes. "Huh?"

He'd taken her purse out of her hand and tossed it onto the couch before she even realized it.

"I'm not letting you go, pooh. You said I could fix this."

Burying her forehead in his chest, Riana toyed with the idea of telling him the truth.

"It's best for you if I leave and we act like we never saw each other in the store, Luca." Lifting her head from his chest, she looked up at him with glossy eyes. "Let me go."

"No." He took her hands into his and began to two step, not caring if she joined him or not. "I freed myself of you once before, and it was the biggest mistake I'd ever made. The second was forcing you to get rid of our baby." Riana tried to remove her hands from his, but he held them tighter. "If you don't want to be with a nigga that's cool, Riana, I get and accept that, but you gon' let me make this right."

"Why!" Riana roared, pushing him back by the chest. "So you can sleep better at night? Fuck you and your amends, Luca. For real." She grabbed her purse again. "You think just because you want to make things right that that's what's going to happen? That does nothing for me, bruh. You hurt me." The tears she'd been holding in began to fall as her bottom lip trembled. Luca's head lowered as he avoided her leaking eyes. Her voice was just above a whisper as she jabbed her heart while saying, "To my *core*." Riana chuckled as she wiped her face. "And you have no idea what you did to me. What you turned me into."

She stormed away, ignoring the sound of Herbert's voice in her head. Riana wasn't sure what she'd have to do to be able to go through with this but playing nice was not it. Luca was so light on his feet she didn't even hear him walking behind her, but when he closed and locked the door behind them she groaned and continued to her car.

As quickly as she was inside of hers was as quickly as Luca was inside of his. He followed her out of his driveway and down the street, and all Riana could do was chuckle. She called him from the Bluetooth in her car, rolling her eyes at the calmness in his tone when he answered.

"Are you following me?"

"...Yea."

"Why?"

"'Cause this conversation ain't over, Santee."

Her speed escalated as she gripped the steering wheel tighter. Needing to revert back to herself, Riana decided it was best if she put as much space between them as possible. Luca wouldn't leave her alone if he felt she was upset, so she had to get out of her feelings and make this right.

"It's cool, Luca. I'm sorry for spazzing and blaming you. This isn't your fault. I chose to mess with you after you made it clear that you didn't want to be in a committed relationship. All I had to do was cut you off and I wouldn't have gotten hurt."

"But you tried to cut me off, pooh. I pursued you. Now

I've already apologized for that and I won't keep spewing those words. I'm trying to show you that I've changed through my actions..."

"I don't want to see the change," Riana admitted to the both of them, yelling so loudly her throat scratched.

She rested her head against the headrest as she remained silent to collect herself. Him being a changed man would make this hard as hell. It would have been easy to do away with the old Luca. The one who put himself above everyone else and didn't give a damn about her feelings if they went against his desires, but this Luca... this Luca was going to be a lot harder to shake.

"There's nothing I can do about that, Riana. I hate that you had to experience that version of me, but I'm not that man anymore. I've changed, and you deserve to experience this version of me. Now pull over."

Riana drove about half a mile before pulling over to the side of the road. She put her car in park, and as if he felt her internal conflict, Herbert called her. Ignoring his call just in time, Riana temporarily blocked his number as Luca opened the door.

Kneeling before her, Luca placed his hand on her knee.

"You don't owe me a second chance, but I owe you, Riana. I owe you, and I'm going to treat you like the valuable treasure you are. You're right; I do need this for my peace, but more importantly, you need it for yours too. I don't want your husband to have to suffer because of what I did to you."

Riana's hands covered her face, but Luca wasted no time pulling them down.

"When Tati called you a fairy, I knew this was destined. You're my fate. The woman who possessed the power and magic to change my life for the better. You were sent to bring me blessings and good luck. To take away my worry. I failed at seeing it in that moment and God blessed me with Tati through Aaliyah, but that was supposed to be you, Riana. Maybe I'm being selfish, but yea, I need to make things right with you."

Riana's head shook as she tried to look away but Luca's hand on her chin kept her from doing so.

"You hear me? I need this, Santee."

"What about what I need?" His grip on her chin loosened. "It's always about what you want and need, Luca. But what about what *I* need?"

He nodded slowly as his hands fell from her. "That's true. What do you want and need?"

Taking a moment to think over his question, Riana allowed herself to consider what she truly wanted and needed in that moment, not just for her contract with Herbert.

"I want you to fix what you broke, but that's not your responsibility." Riana cupped his cheek and massaged it with her thumb. "It's mine. I need you to understand that you can't force me to let you treat me right after you've done me wrong. It's not fair, Luca. Right now, I see a small glimpse of the new man that you've become, but more than anything, I see that night over and over again. I feel that pain over and over again..."

"Then let me take it away. Just trust me, Riana. If I can't fix this and make you feel better I swear I'll leave you alone, but you gotta give me a chance."

Even if that wasn't what she wanted personally, it was what she needed professionally. This was a job. Luca was a mark. And Riana would need not to blur the lines. She would need not to allow her newfound overflow of emotions to keep her from getting close and gaining enough of his trust to strike.

"Okay," Riana agreed softly.

Luca's head tilted, and Riana could literally see the ache in his heart over her agreement. He smiled softly before brushing it away with a lick of his lips.

"Cool. Cool. Give me your phone."

Riana unlocked her phone and handed it to him. He opened iTunes, and as soon as "Love and Happiness" began to play Riana smiled, genuinely this time. Luca helped her get out of the car, and on the side of the road, they began to dance.

One song turned into three. Three turned into five. And by then, revenge, contracts, and Herbert held no space in her mind.

As Luca held her close and lowered his lips to hers, Riana gave him access with no reservations. Before she could fully surrender to feeling his lips again, the flashing of blue lights caused them to separate.

"Get in your car. I got this," Luca ordered, and Riana

was so used to leading it took her a second to do as he said, but when she did, she got into her car and closed the door.

As Luca talked to the officer, who was probably being more nosy than anything, Riana took her phone off of do not disturb. Glancing over several missed calls from Amigo, she assumed they were really from Herbert. She shot him a simple three-word text, hoping that would get him off her back.

I'm handling it.

Luca opened her door and confirmed her suspicions when he said, "He's been in the cut over there for the past hour or so and was just being nosy." Riana smiled, unsure of what to say or do at this point. "What do you want and need, Santee? You ready to call it a night? Or you coming back home with me?"

"What do you want?"

"It's not about what I want."

"Yes, it is. I want you to be mindful of what I want and need, but your wants and needs matter too."

"I'm confident they will align if we're on the same page. What do you want, Santee?"

It wasn't as difficult of a choice as Riana thought it would be.

"I want to go home with you, and I need you to not give up on me."

UNTITLED

"Just call me a thief
She was on top of me
Then I left with her heart
Broken and scarred
Made no apologies"

uca

LUCA DIDN'T KNOW who he wanted to look at more, Tatiana as she jumped up and down in excitement or Riana as she skipped over to her while she giggled. It was time for him to drop Tatiana off at the airport so she could go back home with Aaliyah, but since he was texting Riana and found out she was at her grandmother's house he decided to pull up on her. He said it was because he was tired of Tatiana asking him about the pretty pink haired fairy from the store, but he wanted to see her himself too.

"Ah!" Tatiana screamed, finally running over to Riana.

Riana squatted, arms open and waiting for Tatiana to enter.

In her five years of living, Luca had never seen Tatiana take to anyone as quickly as Riana. She was a naturally friendly and loving child, but her connection with Riana was different, and it was one that couldn't be ignored. Not even if Luca wanted to.

"Hey, doll face," Riana spoke, smiling up at him with shining eyes.

This was the second time she'd seen her since Tatiana had been in Memphis this past week, and every time they saw each other they were twice as excited as the time before.

"Hey, Ms. Ari. Are you riding with my daddy to take me to the airport?"

Tatiana had made it clear that she was going to ask that, but Luca wasn't sure what Riana's answer would be. Although he had to see to business after he dropped Tatiana off, Luca would never pass up the chance to spend time with Riana. Over the past week, she'd been trying to give him as open of a chance as she possibly could. But there were times, and she had those days, where nothing he would do or say was right. Even with her inconsistency, Luca knew making things right with her was worth it.

"I think your daddy has to work after he drops you off, doll face, but I can't wait for you to come back so I can see you again."

Riana pinched Tatiana's cheek, causing her to blush and giggle before hugging Riana again. Hand in hand, they walked over to the car. After Riana made sure Tatiana was buckled up safely, she made her way over to Luca's side of the car. He grabbed the flowers he'd purchased for her off the seat and her feet stopped moving as soon as she saw them.

"Come on give me a hug so I can go, crazy."

With the cutest pout Luca had seen, Riana slowly walked over to him. He gave her the flowers before taking her into his arms.

"They're beautiful, Luca. Thank you."

"Thank you for being so nice to my daughter. She's crazy about you, and that makes me even more crazy about you."

"She's the cutest little thing in life." Riana lowered her arms from around his neck, but Luca kept her at his chest. "A part of me…" Her head shook as she pulled herself away from him, and Luca hoped she didn't switch up on him. "Sometimes I wondered why I wasn't good enough to have your baby." Riana's jaw clenched as she looked away. "And then I see you with her." Her eyes focused on Tatiana, and she smiled as she waved at her. "And she's so beautiful and sweet and…" Riana returned her eyes to Luca. "That girl is perfect, and I know you think it was meant to be me… but she's perfect, Luca, and that's because of you and Aaliyah."

"I know this might make us losing our baby harder…"

"We didn't lose our baby, Luca." Riana closed the space between them and whispered, "I killed him or her," as her tears began to fall. "Because that's what you wanted, and I wanted to make you happy, because I wanted you to make *me* happy. But I have to be happy with myself."

Looking over her head to avoid her eyes, Luca's hand

wrapped around the side of her neck. He used it lay her head against his chest. His arms encircled her, and he placed the bottom of his chin on the top of her head.

"I don't want to make you relive this every time you see us, Riana. If you need me to let you go, I will. I wish I knew how to help you heal, but I don't know what to do, pooh. If you can tell me I swear I will, but I don't know what to do."

"It's not fair to you," she sobbed, then chuckled. "I've cried and felt more this past week than I have in years. It's clear that you've changed, and I don't want to punish you because of your old ways." Riana stepped back, wiping her face as she avoided his eyes. "I just think that, it would be for the best, if we stopped this while we're ahead." She looked at him. Finally. Riana took his hand into hers. "I really appreciate all you've done. You don't know how good you trying to make things right makes me feel. But we should go our separate ways."

As much as Luca didn't want to agree, he didn't want to force what he wanted on her more. Grabbing her chin, he placed a kiss to the center of her forehead before agreeing with, "Whatever you need, Santee."

She stepped back, giving him the space necessary to get into his car. He told himself not to look back as he drove away, but he couldn't resist. And the sad look on her face was one Luca wouldn't forget.

UNTITLED

"We can be so hollow
Like my rib cage, the echoes follow
Follow me like the fears I swallow
And drown in all my mistakes"

uca

THERE WAS NO DENYING IT; Herbert not only had a price on Luca's head, but he'd also given the job to the Femme Fatale. Everyone in the streets knew of her reputation. She killed every mark and executed every contract. Although there was no fear in his heart, the confirmation had Luca more aware of how important it was to spend as much time as he possibly could with his daughter and his family. He didn't plan on allowing any new women to get close to him, but if she was on his trail, she'd strike regardless, and if Luca's time was coming to an end he wanted to make sure his family knew he loved them and would continue to watch over them.

When Riana called things off a few hours ago Luca was admittedly disappointed, but now he figured that was for the best. The last thing he wanted to do was make her fall in love with him again just to walk out of her life all over again... even if it was through death.

Wanting to feel close to her, Luca went down to the Mississippi River, where they'd spent numerous nights walking and talking. He saw her from behind first. A part of him wanted to leave, but the other part of him felt drawn to her. Shoving his hands into his pockets, Luca slowly walked over to Riana. He stood directly behind her, and before he could make his presence known she asked...

"Everything okay with business?"

Luca wrapped his arms around her, and as soon as he did she topped them with hers.

"As okay as it can be."

Riana released a tired sigh, and Luca couldn't help placing a soft kiss to her temple.

"I don't want to be stupid, Luca. I don't want to let you hurt me again. I love you so much it feels like you could do anything to me and I'd still love you, and I can't be that fool again."

Luca turned her in his arms. "I understand, Riana. Completely. That's love, pooh. You risk being a fool for a nigga that can do you wrong. But you gotta trust me when I say that ain't me no more." Her head began to turn away, but Luca clutched her chin and stopped it. "Hear me; I will never do anything to intentionally hurt you again. I put that on my daughter.

But I can't be bringing you into her life if you don't plan on sticking around. She doesn't deserve to be hurt because of my past mistakes. If you're going to give me a genuine chance to show you that I can treat you right this time around cool. If not, this ends permanently tonight. I have no time to waste, Santee. So what do you want?"

There was no part of Luca that wanted to be rejected twice in the same day, especially after the news he'd just gotten, but it was best to get it over with now than to drag this on.

Riana's arms wrapped around his neck as she whispered, "I want you, Luca. I'm not saying it's going to be easy but..."

Luca silenced her by covering her lips with his. No, it wouldn't be easy, but she was willing to try, and that was more than enough for him.

UNTITLED

"All I know is if my skin bled
Like the ink dripped from my pen
My bed will be drenched in a scarlet rose red
And drown in all my mistakes"

CHAPTER 13

 he Past
Riana

RIANA SHOULD HAVE KNOWN it was a set up. She should have known Luca's sister, Ladia, was up to something when she wanted to become her friend, but she had so few female friends that Riana decided to go for it anyway. Of Luca's two siblings, Ladia and Leonard, Riana naturally assumed she'd vibe best with Leonard, but Luca wasn't having that. About two weeks passed and her and Ladia had hung out a few times before Ladia invited Riana to her house. Except it wasn't just her house. It was her second home. Luca's home.

Ladia opened the door and told her to follow the trail of rose petals before hugging Riana tightly and leaving. She started to leave, but since Luca had gone through all of this trouble, she figured the least she could do was hear him out.

Following the trail of rose petals led to the balcony, where Luca stood waiting for her. Dressed in all white, he was the spitting image of temptation. The closer Riana got to him, the weaker her resolve became. As much as she hated to admit it, no man made her feel the way Luca did. No man pursued her the way Luca did. No man spoiled her the way Luca did.

Had it not been for his inability to commit, he would have been perfect.

On top of the table were chocolate covered strawberries, pineapples, and grapes, along with a bottle of champagne. He had a portable DVD player on the table as well, alongside candles and a few sprinkled rose petals.

"What are you doing, Luca?"

"Trying to get my woman back." Luca took her by the hand and pulled her into his chest. "I miss you, Santee."

"You wouldn't have to miss me if..."

Luca's nostrils flared as his thumb caressed her lips. After kissing her gently, Luca propositioned her with, "Give me one month." Riana's head shook as she removed herself from his grip, but he continued. "We're young, pooh. You have plenty of time to get serious, get married, and have babies. Let's just have fun right now. All I'm asking for is a month. If you don't want to rock with me no more after that, I'll cut you loose."

Her mind didn't want her to, but Riana's heart considered his request.

"You can have your pick of any woman..."

"But I want you."

She nibbled on her bottom lip gently, trying to convince herself of another excuse.

"I'm not even worth all of this."

"Yes, you are, and the fact that you aren't aware of that lets me know you need someone like me to help you figure that out."

Riana chuckled as she headed for the sliding door.

"Oh, so I'm worth this, but I'm not worth commitment? Miss me with the bullshit, Luca."

"It's not bullshit. Me not wanting commitment has absolutely nothing to do with your worth. Me not wanting commitment is my personal choice. All I'm asking for is one month, Riana. You can't spare that?"

She could, and she would, but Riana prayed that choice was one she wouldn't regret.

UNTITLED

"Skin on my skin, what a wonderful sin
Take your breath but you're asking for more
The tip of my finger is tracing your figure
I say good night and walk out the door"

CHAPTER 14

iana

THIS TIME when tears filled Riana's eyes, they were happy tears. Proud tears. Pushing them back, she turned around to grab the bag that Luca was walking over to her to get. It was Saturday afternoon, and instead of resting, he'd spent the start of his day going from nursing homes to homeless shelters. He'd entertained and listened to the old, then edified and fed the young and struggling.

There was no denying it at this point – Luca Kareem was a changed man. One who put others above himself. One who took into consideration the feelings and needs of others. One who wanted to do more good than harm. One who didn't deserve death.

Two weeks had passed since Riana agreed to giving

them a genuine chance, and things were going a lot smoother than she expected. The war she thought she'd be at with her heart and mind wasn't there. It didn't matter how much she tried to remind her heart of the pain she'd sustained... how much she tried fill her mind with hypothetical worry of Luca hurting her again... his words and actions in the present were too good to allow her to trick any part of her to worry about something bad.

If anything, she felt bad about herself. About her choice. About the contract. Here Luca was, trying his hardest to build her up while she was in position to tear him down.

And Tatiana.

Poor little Tatiana.

The thought of her losing her father at the hands of Riana literally caused her to be sick to her stomach.

"You ready?" Luca asked, pulling Riana out of her thoughts. She hadn't even realized he'd given out the last bag of food and returned to his place next to her.

With a nod, Riana placed her hand inside of his and they walked back to his car. Luca didn't pull off right away, giving Riana time to feel comfortable asking, "Why do you spend your Saturday's doing this?"

Luca smiled as he started his car.

"I've taken so much from my city, this is how I give back. Feeding the old and young however they need it. Tomorrow morning, I'll be back at the nursing home with a van to take whoever wants to go to church. However they need to be fed, Santee."

As he pulled out of the parking lot, he told her about the

fitness classes he sponsored at the nursing home and the shopping runs he took them on and had a team of college students to do for those who weren't able to leave but didn't have family seeing to their needs. He also told her about the hotels he partnered with to give the homeless shelter when it was really cold, really hot, or raining. For quite a few, he'd helped them find jobs by providing them with an address to use and transportation.

The entire time he talked Riana's heart broke. She wouldn't just be pulling Luca from his daughter; she'd be pulling him from an entire community. Sure, he dabbled in illegal dealings, selling that herb whose high could bring people low, but Riana could see no flaw in Luca in that moment – only herself.

Justifying it by saying she signed the contract before she became aware of the new him didn't make her feel any better. Not at all. All it did was make her feel like a coward for not taking responsibility.

"I'm proud of you, baby. I didn't think you'd become all that you have, and..." She was about to say she couldn't wait to see who he became in the future, but he didn't have one. Not past the next two months. "I'm just really proud of you, Luca."

Luca took her hand into his. He placed a tender kiss to it.

"Honestly, Santee, I wish I could say I want you at my side while I continue on." Riana looked over at him as his head shook. "I want you, more than you know, but I don't think it's fair to commit to you. And I'm not saying that because I'm out here fucking around; I'm saying that because I don't know how much time I have left. While I'd love to spend the rest of my days with my daughter and you, it just... doesn't seem fair committing to you knowing I could die soon."

Even though she knew full well, Riana asked, "What do you mean?"

She listened as Luca told her about Herbert, their family history, and how he'd put a price on his head. Not just a price on his head, but one that the Femme Fatale was going to collect. He'd assured her that she didn't have to worry about him entertaining any other women but that that wouldn't stop her from hitting her mark. It never did.

"I don't want you to worry about me," Luca assured her before kissing her hand again. "I'm heavily protected and I know how to move. But I'm not invincible, and when it's my time it'll be my time."

Riana nodded, swallowing back tears. These tears, they were sad tears again.

"Do me a solid, though," Luca requested, to which Riana looked over at him intently. "Don't let nobody come to my funeral crying over me knowing I ain't fuck with them. And don't let them sing no sad songs either. I want that hoe to be a party. Send 'em to church. I'm talking about have them..."

Luca released the wheel, shut his eyes, and began to dance and shout in his seat as if he was at church and had caught the Holy Ghost.

"Luca!" Riana yelled through her laugh, grabbing the wheel. "You better stop before He gets you for real!"

Luca opened his eyes and grabbed the wheel as Riana continued to laugh until she cried.

"That's what I wanted to see," he confessed, licking away the remnants of his smile.

"What?"

"Your smile. Stop looking sad over there. Ima be good, and even when I'm not good..." He pointed up towards the sky. "I'll be good."

Riana's smile fell but she tried to put it back to put his mind at ease.

"And... you want to spend your time with... me?"

Luca chuckled, amused by her skepticism.

"Who else would I want to be with besides Riana Santee? You've always been it for me. And you're starting to love my daughter, and she already loves you. There's no one else I'd rather spend my time with, whether I have ten days, ten years, or ten eternities. I want them with you, pooh."

"Then if that's the case..." Riana unbuckled her seatbelt. "I want us to have it all."

She climbed over to his side of the car, and Luca wasted no time pulling over to the side of the road. Thankfully, his windows were tinted, but at this point, neither of them really gave a damn.

"Are you sure, Riana? I don't want to have you just to leave you again." His head rested against the headrest as his fingers slid down her arms. "Can't hurt you again. I refuse to hurt you again."

Riana's head lowered. She took his neck into her hands and kissed him softly.

"I'm sure. This is what I want."

Luca smiled with one side of his mouth. "Then I'm yours and yours alone. And you're mine."

He pulled her back down to his lips with one hand while pushing her maxi dress up with the other...

UNTITLED

"Put that on my life, everything I love
Never crossed no line
It was all because I dedicate my life
To lovin' you right
Love comes before pride, I loved you before I
'Fore I even knew why"

iana

RIANA BROKE their kiss to request, "I need to hear you say it, Luca. I've waited eight years for this."

Luca smiled softly, running his fingers through her hair.

"You're my woman, and I'm your man. From this day forward, we're in a committed relationship. My heart bleeds and beats for Tatiana Kareem, but it belongs to Riana Santee."

She placed her forehead on his, unsure of how she'd be able to go through with the hit. There was no way she could kill this man. Not after all of this. But what other choice did she have? She'd signed the contract, and there was no way in hell Herbert was going to let her out of it – not without a life for a life.

Luca lifted his head and connected his lips with hers, instantly clearing her mind of anxiety and the worry that was filling her. And just as easily as he emptied her Luca filled her, reminding her that he had always been and would probably be the best lover she'd ever had. A quiet moan fell from her lips as she took all of him in, allowing him to touch the bottom of her pussy.

"I missed you so much, baby."

Her eyes were locked with his, though they were growing lower each time she lifted herself to the top of his shaft and slid back down again.

"I missed you, pooh. And I missed being in this pussy too. She fits me like she was made for me."

Luca pushed his seat back further, then leaned her forward, angling her in a way that allowed him to hit her spot with each stroke. Why did he know how to please her so well? Why did he know *her* so well? Well, there was one thing he didn't know, and Riana prayed he never found out.

"I love you, Riana."

Her tightly sealed eyes opened to look into his. For a few seconds, she couldn't even reply. Couldn't open her mouth because if she did she'd probably cry. Instead she lowered herself to his and kissed him. And when she felt like she could handle the truth, she replied with, "I love you too."

With him completely inside, Riana began to rock her hips and squeeze. Not only was she pleasuring herself to the max, but the smacking of her juices covering his shaft was just slightly louder than his quiet moans, letting her know that he was satisfied too. Feeling her walls tighten against him, Riana lifted herself and continued to ride, bouncing up and down with slow, hard, force – what had become the perfect combination for the both of them.

"Riana," he groaned, grabbing her hips and trying to speed her up. When she kept her slow pace, Luca began to lift himself to stroke her faster, but that only made her clench him tighter. "Santee." Her hand went to his neck, and she squeezed gently as her orgasm began to overtake her. "Unless you want to give Tati a sibling you better cum quick."

She laughed, but it quickly turned into a moan as she jerked against him. When her orgasm subsided, she lifted herself, stroking Luca with her hand until he no longer had seeds to spill. After cleaning him off with her tongue, Riana climbed back up to continue her ride since he was still hard.

Maybe she shouldn't have stopped. Maybe she should have given herself the opportunity to have a piece of him forever.

UNTITLED

"How did we get away from love?
How did love get away from us?
Not my time, I should wait for love
Waste of time, what a waste of love"

uca

IT TOOK A LITTLE RESEARCH, but Luca was able to find out what movie was playing in the exact same movie theater he took Riana to for their first date eight years ago. She didn't realize what he was up to until they went to the mall. To the same store. And once she had her arm weighed down with dresses to try on... the same dressing room.

"Luca Kareem, what are you up to?"

His smile was sly as he helped her hang the dresses up.

"The first date we had didn't end as planned, so I was hoping we could change that this time around."

"You're seriously recreating our first date?" Riana's head

shook as he nodded. "You're the best. Get out so we can get to the sex."

Luca laughed as she pushed him out of the dressing room. Anxiously he waited to see how everything looked on her. Like eight years ago, the first dress she tried on was white. The second was black. But the third was pink.

"Wha'chu doing?" Luca asked, sitting up in his seat.

Riana shrugged innocently. "What do you mean?"

"You got seventy red dresses in there. Put one of them hoes on."

Playfully rolling her eyes, Riana did a slow spin as she smiled. "You don't like this one, baby?"

"Yea, but I like the red ones better."

Her hands went to her hips as she chuckled. "How do you know? You haven't even seen them on me yet."

"Put one on then."

"Fine."

Riana closed the door behind her, leaving Luca alone to return his attention to his phone. His current priority was to move as much of his money around as he possibly could. He already had a will created because of his illegal lifestyle, but now he was in the process of moving funds from offshore accounts so those he wanted to continue to take care of would be able to access them easily. Although his plan was to find and do away with the Femme Fatale before she could bring any harm to him, Luca had always been a logical and realistic man.

No threats on his life were ever pushed under the rug,

no matter who they came from or who they were supposed to be carried out by.

When the door opened again, Luca looked up from his phone, groaning at the gold dress Riana had on. It was sexy, and he liked it a lot, but nothing looked as good as red did against her skin.

"Why you trying me?" Luca asked, putting his phone in his pocket and standing to his feet. "I see you're in the mood to play."

Riana laughed until he stepped into the dressing room and closed the door behind him. Then, that laughter turned into a smile. Turning her back to him, Riana looked at him through the mirror.

"Undress me."

Standing behind her, Luca pushed her hair over her left shoulder and kissed the right side of her neck. His hands went to her breasts, and he massaged her already hard nipples. Roaming her body, his hands landed on the bottom of the dress. Luca lifted it up just enough to see his favorite part of her. Sliding his hand into her panties, Luca massaged her clit with his middle and ring finger. Her head tilted as she held the back of his head, keeping him on her spot on her neck.

The doorknob jiggled before someone whispered, "Oops. Someone's in this one."

Riana turned towards him with a smile. She wrapped her arms around his neck as she suggested, "Why don't we go get something to eat and finish this at your place? I want you in bed. We can make new memories there." Luca opened his mouth, but before he could ask Riana added, "And I'll put on a red dress."

UNTITLED

"You became my life, put that on my life
Took me out my mind, took my peace of mind
I never realized you were my light
Without you by my side, that just don't
feel right"

iana

"ASK ME AGAIN."

There was no need for Riana to ask Luca to clarify. They were at the same seafood restaurant from years ago, and with him trying to right his wrongs, that conversation was where the shift began. Riana took a sip of her white wine before inhaling a deep breath. She swallowed hard, shutting all of the other voices and conversations out that were happening around them.

"What are your intentions with me?"

Luca reached across the table for her hand, and Riana happily obliged.

"I intend to love you, cherish you, honor you, and be faithful to you for the rest of my life." Riana caressed his hand with her thumb as she nibbled on her bottom lip. "My goal is to take care of the Femme Fatale before she takes care of me. If I can, I intend to marry you and give you babies. I know that doesn't fix what I made you do..."

"No." That bitter smile made its way across her face as she covered his hand with her free one. "That was my choice." Luca's head shook but Riana didn't allow him to speak. "You wanted me to get the abortion, but you didn't force me to do anything I didn't want to do."

He could sense the change in her emotions, so Luca said, "We don't have to talk about this, pooh."

"I need this," *in more ways than you know,* "Because I've blamed you for so much, and that wasn't fair. I wanted my baby, yes, but more than that, I didn't want a baby with a man who didn't want it or me. It was going to be torture raising a baby that looked like you without you. And even if you were in the baby's life, I knew in my heart that you wouldn't be mine. So I blamed it on you, but that was my choice too. Just like it was my choice to become..."

Riana snapped her mouth shut quickly, refusing to reveal who she really was. Or the fact that she'd blamed him for turning her into the heartless, ruthless woman she'd become. But for the first time in years, Riana was finally accepting the part she'd played in her hearts demise.

"You were honest with me about everything, Luca. I'm the one that chose to be with you. I chose to hurt from loving you instead of hurt by letting you go, and the abortion among other things was my punishment for that. But I don't want you to blame yourself for that anymore. That was *our* choice. We have to learn from it and let it go."

Luca stared at her for a while before nodding and pulling his hand from under hers.

They remained silent until their food arrived. Once it did, conversation sparked after asking each other how their dishes tasted.

With a mouth full of succulent crab, Riana managed to get out, "I have a game for us to play when dinner is over."

Luca chuckled as she swallowed, and the moment reminded her of the first day they met. When he picked her up from her home, he took her out to eat. It was her first time getting high, and she experienced every side effect to the max. From finding everything hilarious and cracking jokes that made Luca laugh to having an appetite out of this world and falling asleep at the table. That night, she fell asleep mid-sentence with a piece of crab in her mouth.

"Why wait? We can start now," Luca suggested, placing another piece of lobster into his mouth.

"Well, it's an intimacy game. You basically ask your partner questions that are supposed to help you know them on a deeper level."

"Cool. What's the first question?"

"What would you do if you knew you could not fail?"

Scratching the side of his face, Luca sat back in his seat as he thought over her question. Took a few seconds, but eventually he answered with, "Get out the game, go to law school, move closer to my baby, and live the good life."

Riana chuckled in disbelief as she wiped her hands.

"What makes you think you would fail at any of that? The Luca I fell in love with was capable of having and doing anything he set his mind to. You always had a comeback and solution to everything. The only person capable of stopping you and making you fail is you, and I refuse to let you play yourself like that."

"That's why you've always been my day one." They shared a small smile, until Luca asked, "How are you, Riana? Really?"

She shrugged and smiled, fully prepared to give the same generic answer she did every time someone asked her how she was doing. But there was something about the way Luca looked at her... something that wouldn't allow her to bullshit him and give him anything less than the truth.

"I could be better, but I've definitely felt worse."

"And what does that mean?"

Riana tapped the top of the table with the tips of her finger, unsure of how much she could say without expressing too much. Until she figured out how she could satisfy Herbert and keep Luca alive, Riana had to be very careful of what she shared and how. Luca had a way of pulling things out of her, and if she said one wrong thing he'd find out the truth in no time.

"Being here with you, like this, feels like heaven. I used to feel so foolish, thinking I loved a man who had no love for me, but I loved you as I much as I did because you did love me. It was just... horrible timing I guess. So I'm happy that we're able to experience this, but there are other things in my life that need to be handled before I can truly be at peace with us."

Luca nodded in understanding. "What can I do to make those things easier for you?"

Now that was an easy question. One that Riana didn't have to put much thought into at all.

"Just be you. The more you love me and remind me of what it feels like to feel... the less those things matter to me."

Putting his glass to his lips, Luca agreed with, "That's something I can most definitely do."

UNTITLED

"Only been a week I think I'm weak can't even
I can't even eat, can't sleep, when we ain't
speakin'
What you telling me boy that's a real weak
reason
You cut me so deep, it hurts for me to
breathe in"

he Past
Riana

IT WASN'T like Luca to not answer Riana's phone calls, and since he was in the streets, her nerves were going to be rattled until she heard from him. She'd stopped by his place and his mother's house and he wasn't at either. Calling Ladia and getting her to call Leonard did nothing. As a last resort, Riana called David hoping he would be with him or had heard from him, but David couldn't offer any answers.

She went to his favorite hangout spots. Still no sight of him.

Finally giving up, Riana decided to head back home, but she wanted to grab something to eat first. She hadn't eaten anything all day, and although she still didn't have much of

an appetite, Riana planned on forcing herself to eat something anyway. It would do her no good to be just as weak
physically as she was emotionally worrying over Luca's
wellbeing.

As soon as Riana stepped foot in the hot wing place she
smelled Luca. Felt him. Even if she couldn't see him. He
was there.

"'Scuse me, lil mama," came from behind her, pulling
Riana out of her thoughts.

"No, excuse me," she replied, stepping to the side so the
man could walk up to the counter.

Looking around, Riana took in every familiar and unfa-
miliar face. Luca was nowhere to be found. Riana released a
hard exhale and made her way to the counter, so she could
order her food. The sound of a door opening from the back
filled Riana's ears. She started to not pay it any mind, but
something told her to have a look. Shifting to the right,
Riana's eyes fell on Luca.

She took a step towards him and opened her mouth to ask
why he hadn't been answering her phone calls, but she stood
frozen, watching as he headed to the table where a woman
sat. Riana's head tilted as she watched Luca's every move.
He slid into the booth next to her and wrapped his arm
around her, smiling when she placed a kiss on his cheek.
Sliding down in his seat, Luca got more comfortable, as if he
hadn't had her worried sick all day.

With a loud huff, Riana stormed over to him, mugging
the back of his head as soon as it was within reach.

"What the fuck, Luca? Seriously? I've been worried sick about your ass all day and you're fucking around with some bitch?"

Luca stood, grabbing her wrists and putting her hands together in an attempt to restrain her as he pushed her away from the table.

"Chill out. You know I don't like attention being drawn to me."

"Then you shouldn't be out fucking around! I've been blowing your phone up thinking something has happened to you and this is what you're doing?"

As sad as Riana wanted to be, in that moment, all she felt was anger. Anger at herself for letting one month turn into three. Anger at Luca for making her think she was the only woman in the world just to turn around and make her feel as if she wasn't enough.

"Why you acting surprised? I told you I didn't want to be in a committed relationship. What did you think that meant?"

Riana chuckled as she fought to remove herself from his grip. "I didn't think it meant you would disrespect me by cheating on me, especially in public."

"How am I cheating on you if we're not in a relationship? I fuck with you tough, but I'm single, Santee. If I want to talk to someone else I can do that. I ain't fucking her, so why you care?"

All of her fire and fight fizzled. Her shoulders slumped as her head lowered. As if he'd realized what he said had the power to hurt her, Luca's voice softened. He went from restraining her by the wrists to trying to hug her, but Riana pushed him away.

"Your month is past up. Since you want her, be with her. Leave me the fuck alone from this point forward, Luca."

She tried to walk away, but Luca grabbed her by the arm. Jerking away from him, Riana's steps out of the restaurant sped up. With Luca right behind her, she avoided the eyes of everyone watching, feeling her chest cave in around her heart.

"Riana." Ignoring his calling of her name, Riana continued to her car. The emptiness that filled her stomach now was for a different reason, one that wouldn't be filled by food. Not physical food at least. She needed to be filled with love, and the man she wanted to fill her was making a fool out of her instead. "I'm sorry, Riana."

Unable to open her car door, Riana squeezed her eyes shut as Luca pressed his body into hers. Pinning her between him and the door, Luca kissed the back of her head.

"I didn't mean to come at you so hard, especially in front of people. I'm sorry, pooh."

"Can you move so I can go?"

"Okay, but I'm coming through tonight so we can talk."

"There's nothing for us to talk about, Luca. You asked for a month and I gave you three. It's clear that you don't plan on committing to me. It's one thing for us to be fucking around with no title and no outside parties, but I'm not going to let you mess around with other women while you have me."

Luca turned her in his direction, but she avoided his eyes.

"So you're going to cut me off? Like what we have doesn't mean shit?"

Riana's eyes widened in disbelief before she laughed. "Yo, something is wrong with you, Luca. For real. Move so I can get in my car. Your little girlfriend is waiting for you."

She pushed him back, putting enough space between them to be able to open the door.

"I don't want her, Riana. I want you."

"Then why are you here with her!" Riana roared, tears starting to fall.

Luca looked away, jaw clenching as he exhaled. "Please don't cry. I never wanted to make you cry over me."

"Let me go then. If you don't want to hurt me, let me go."

He looked at her briefly as she wiped her face, nodding softly. "Okay." Stuffing his hands in his pockets, Luca watched as she got into her car. But she couldn't start it. Couldn't drive away. A part of her wanted him to apologize and vow to make this right, and Luca sensed that because he opened her door, unbuckled her seatbelt, and pulled her into his arms. "I'm sorry, pooh. I promise you I don't want her. We can leave right now."

"No. Do you not understand how scared I was when I couldn't get a hold of you? I seriously thought something had happened to you, and you were ignoring my calls because..."

Pushing him away, Riana hopped back into her car. She slammed the door behind her, locking it so he wouldn't be able to get to her that easily again. With tears streaming *down her cheeks, Riana started her car and sped off. Yes, she wanted him to make this right, but that desire felt... so... wrong.*

UNTITLED

"How did we get away from love?
How did love get away from us?
Not our time, we should wait for love
Waste of time, what a waste of love
You're my wasted love"

iana

"Just one more," Luca pleaded. "Stop sticking your gum out, Tati. Smile."

Both Riana and Tatiana rolled their eyes, and as soon as they did Luca frowned, causing them both to giggle. Tatiana was back in Memphis for the weekend. For the first two days, Riana gave them their time alone – even though she was missing Tatiana like crazy and anxious to spend time with her. Today, the trio had been together ever since they woke up.

Their day started with breakfast, courtesy of Riana. After that, she took Tatiana for a girls' spa day. It ended with her giving Tatiana temporary streaks of pink in her hair. She'd fallen in love with the color, and Riana was sure she'd have a fit when they washed it out of her hair later that night.

After her mini makeover, they went shopping for identical outfits, allowing Luca to join in on the fun by wearing the same color as them.

They had an early dinner, then went to Incredible Pizza. After staying for hours, they were hungry all over again. All three feasted on pizza before heading back home. They all changed into matching onesies and watched a couple of movies with candy and popcorn. Now that the day was almost over, Tatiana was ready to go to sleep, but Luca wanted to get as many pictures as he possibly could.

"Daddy," Tatiana whined, wrapping her arms around Riana and hugging her from the side. "I'm so sleepy I'm about to fall overrrrrr."

"Awwww," Riana whined herself, picking Tatiana up. "That's enough, Luca. Let her go to sleep."

"Fine," Luca grumbled, snapping a few more pictures. "Make sure she spits that gum out," he added to the back of her as she carried Tatiana down the hall.

Pulling the comforter back, Riana chuckled at the sound of Tatiana's breathing growing harder already.

"Yea, it's way past your bedtime, doll face."

She put her into the middle of the bed as gently as she possibly could and covered her with the comforter. Once she was sure Tatiana was tucked in securely, Riana placed a kiss to her forehead.

"Goodnight, Tati. Sweet dreams."

"Goodnight, Mommy," Tatiana replied, turning to her side.

Riana remained frozen, staring down at Tatiana until she heard her light snores.

Mommy.

Where did that come from?

Convinced it was sleep causing Tatiana to confuse her with Aaliyah, Riana tried to brush it off as she left the room. She didn't do as good of a job as she thought because Luca asked, "What's wrong?" as he cut the TV off.

"Nothing. Just..." Riana paused as she grabbed the empty bowl that was once full of popcorn. "I'm sure it was just a mistake. Because she was tired."

"What?"

"Tati called me mommy when I told her goodnight."

Luca smiled softly, walking out of the living room to the kitchen. Riana followed behind hesitantly.

"I'm not surprised," was all he said.

Leaning against the island, Riana waited for him to continue. But he didn't. "Luca."

He chuckled quietly as he put the bowl in the sink. As usual, Riana went behind him to wash it instead of letting it sit there overnight.

"Yesterday when I was trying to find her something to wear to go and see my momma she got a little attitude because she didn't like what I picked, so she asked where her mommy was so she could put her together a better outfit. I told her Aaliyah was not about to hop on a plane to go through her closet, but that we could FaceTime her. She told me she was talking about her mommy in Memphis. Of course I knew she was talking about you, but I asked her who she was talking about anyway."

Luca came and stood next to Riana at the sink. What started as her washing the bowl turned into her letting the water flow over her empty hands.

"She said she was talking about Riana. Her fairy." Riana's head lowered as her eyes watered. "I made it clear to her that Aaliyah is her mother, and no one could take her place, but that you were a mother figure to her. That if I played my cards right, one day you would legally be her second mother." Luca turned her in his direction. "Her mother in love. A mother that chose to love her, even though she didn't have to. She said okay, but clearly she's going to call you what she wants. We're both lucky to have you, Riana."

Riana nodded, removing herself from his grip. Her tears were threatening to pour, and while Luca may have assumed she was in her feelings with happiness, there was a deep singe of pain there too. If Tatiana ever found out about her betrayal, there would be nothing she could do to repair their relationship. She wasn't setting herself up to lose just Luca, she was setting herself up to lose Tatiana too. And as she grew closer to her, that became just as much of an unbearable thought as losing Luca.

"If you want me to tell her not to call you that..."

"No, it's..." Riana cut the water off and dried her hands. "I don't want her to feel like how she feels about me is wrong. It just caught me off guard. That's all. And I never want Aaliyah to think I'm trying to take her place."

"Look at me, Riana." She did. "Aaliyah doesn't think that. I talked to her about it as soon as it happened, and she's happy that I'm with someone that Tati approves of. She does want to meet you, but we can set that up for a later time. Neither of us has a problem sharing Tatiana with you. It makes me proud to know that she's so fond of you. As long as you're comfortable, we're good."

Riana nodded as she made her way into his arms.

She'd set out for revenge.

To get her heart back.

To remove it from Luca's possession.

But the more time she spent with him, the more she gained. Tatiana was at the top of that list, and Riana was sure of one thing – she'd protect Tatiana's heart at all costs. She'd give her own life before she let Herbert or anyone else take Luca from her.

UNTITLED

"You're confused so you
Do not know the truth"

uca

LUCA PAID no attention to the road as he stared at the picture. He was on his way back home from a trip to Miami, and he was missing Riana so much all he could do was go through their text messages and look at the pictures of her in his phone. They'd been back in each other's lives for a month and a half, and she'd become such an integral part of his day and life that spending three days away from her felt like hell on earth. But that was a part of his business. At any given moment, shit could go left, and he had to take care of it immediately.

The supplier he'd been using for the past two years was

arrested, and Luca not only had to make sure he understood the severity of snitching and naming names, but he also had to find a new supplier. This weekend had been a bloody, busy mess, and he couldn't wait to get home and between Riana's legs.

Unable to resist, Luca called her, hoping she would answer. It was close to four A.M., and that was an hour before Riana woke up to do her morning ritual. She'd been spending the night at his place every night he wasn't at hers, and Luca thoroughly enjoyed getting to know her in that capacity. She answered after the fifth ring, and sleep was thick in her voice.

"Everything okay, baby?"

"Yea. Just wanted to hear your voice. I'm on my way home."

"Yaayyyyy."

Luca chuckled quietly, not wanting to wake up the guard that was sleeping next to him.

"We're about forty-five minutes out. After we all get back to our cars, I'll be on my way home to you."

"I can't wait. I've missed you so much, Luca."

"I've missed you t—"

"Dro! Wake the fuck up, bro!" Kel yelled from the front passenger seat, gaining Luca's attention immediately.

Dro's head lifted immediately, but it was too late. He'd fallen asleep behind the wheel, and the truck had swerved into the left lane. Bright lights blurred Luca's vision as he lowered the phone from his ear. Luca realized they were driving on the wrong side of the road.

"Dro, swerve!" Luca ordered, but it was too late.

Dro tried to get them back into the right lane, but the car plowed into the left side of them.

Luca's side.

UNTITLED

"Listen to your heart, wish you knew your heart
Wish you knew what it sound like
Wish you knew what it felt like
Wish you knew I was down for life
Wish you really was 'bout that life
Wish you knew I was the one
Wish you knew what you wanted"

CHAPTER 21

uca

THIS WAS the fifth time Luca woke up in pain. He hadn't
gone to the hospital, so he didn't have anything strong to
take. While waiting for one of his corner boys to bring him a
bottle of Morphine, Luca tried to sleep to not feel pain, but
that wasn't working. It took what felt like forever for him to
get to sleep, and as soon as he would, the throbbing pain
would have him right back up.

He'd been trying his hardest not to vocalize the
torturous throbbing but moaning and groaning was out of
his control at this point, and every time he did it Riana was
rushing to his side.

"Will you please go to the hospital, Luca?"

"I'm good. As soon as I get these pills I'll be straight."

"What do you think that's going to do in the long run? Your arm could be broken. It's not going to heal. All those pills are going to do is temporarily numb the pain. You need to go to the hospital, Luca."

Luca closed his eyes, as if that would drown out her voice. When the car hit them, the impact was directly on his side. It caused the car to flip over onto the opposite side, but the damage had already been done. He had a nasty gash from when the window burst, and his whole left side was in pain. Nothing hurt worse than his arm, though.

"It's not broken."

"How do you know? You can't even straighten it out."

That was true, but Luca wasn't going to admit that. He wasn't wearing a seatbelt, so as soon as the car flipped he was folded, smashing into Alex who was seated next to him.

"I'm fine, Santee."

With a roll of her eyes, Riana pinched the bridge of her nose. She only did that when she was irritated. Luca couldn't help but smile at the thought of her being irritated because she cared about him. His smile turned into a laugh, but that quickly turned into a groan because of the pain.

"See! You need to go to the hospital. Please, Luca."

"I'm good."

Growling under her breath, Riana stormed away. He heard the water cut on and figured she was running him a bath. Now was one of the times Luca regretted selling only marijuana. A blunt could only make him feel so good. It took the pain away during the high, but it seemed to make things hurt twice as bad when it was over. He'd smoked three blunts already and had given up on the herbs healing effects. Now, his only hope was the morphine pills.

He hated reaching out to his competition, but it was the only way he could get them without a prescription. The good thing about getting the pills from Carl, though, was that there was an unspoken respect between the two men. Luca didn't have to worry about Carl spreading his business or trying to strike and takeover his territory because he thought Luca was out of commission.

Luca's eyes weakened, but before he could drift back to sleep Riana was returning.

"Get up. You need to soak."

Riana helped him out of bed, as slowly and carefully as she possibly could. They took their time walking to the bathroom, and each hunched over step that Luca took felt like it pushed a million tiny needles into his left leg. Lord knows he was trying his hardest not to put much weight on it and limp. If Riana knew that was hurting too, she'd really try to get him to the hospital.

Instead of putting him through the pain of trying to undress himself, Riana cut his clothing off piece by piece. The whole time she did, Luca stared at her, wondering what he'd done over the years to please God so much that he decided to bless him with her all over again.

Luca may not have seen the error in his ways years ago, but as he aged and matured and raised his daughter he became fully aware of how fucked up he'd treated Riana. How he almost destroyed her. Broke not just her heart but her spirit too. Made her feel as if she wasn't enough when she was more than enough. Made her feel as if she wasn't worthy of love when she deserved it more than anyone else.

And after all of that, here she was, taking care of him.

As if he hadn't broken those places inside of her that couldn't be seen. That were harder than anything to be fixed.

Just the thought of God's grace had his eyes watering. He swallowed hard as Riana helped him over to the tub. One by one, she lifted his legs and helped him get inside. The warm water soothed him almost instantly. Riana climbed in behind him, allowing him to rest his back on her chest.

"How does this feel?" she asked softly, squeezing a sponge and allowing the water to trickle down his chest. "It's not too hot is it?"

"It's just right, pooh. Thank you."

Riana let quite a while pass before saying, "I really want you to go see about yourself, Luca."

"No."

"I know you're in more pain than you're telling me. You couldn't even feed yourself this morning. Are you willing to suffer like this for God only knows how long just to avoid going to the hospital?"

"Yea," Luca answered with no hesitation.

Riana laughed, which made him smile.

"I can't stand you sometimes. I'm being serious, Luca."

"I am too. I don't do hospitals. You know that."

She knew that well, too. He'd gotten shot years ago, and

the only reason they got him to the hospital was because he'd lost so much blood and was in so much pain that he passed out. Had he woken up before they made it, Riana was sure he would have made them take him back home.

Luca couldn't describe or explain his reasoning behind loathing hospitals as much as he did. It wasn't a fear. More like an issue of pride. For a man who once thought he was invincible, things like broken hearts and getting shot reminded him that he wasn't.

Even with the price on his head, Luca couldn't succumb fully to the thought of his life being over soon. He'd been trying his hardest and using all of his resources to find out who the Femme Fatale was so he could take care of her before she took care of him. He'd even gone as far as trying to arrange a sit down between him and Herbert, but that was a no go.

Logically, Luca was wise enough to be at peace with his life ending when the time came. But it was the fight, the fighter in him, that wouldn't allow him to bow down to man or death easily. Riana would be the only human being Luca would bow to, and that was only when he asked for her hand in marriage.

"I'm asking you to do it for me. Will you do me that solid, baby? Please?"

Luca thought over her request as he allowed the warm water and her arms around him to relax him.

"What do I get in exchange?"

"You mean besides your health and strength?"

A smile covered his face as he said, "Yea."

"I'll give you a foot massage and a five-minute back scratch."

Her offer, though tempting, wasn't enough. Riana *hated* feet, so for her to be offering to touch his...

"That sounds good, but it's not good enough." Luca turned slightly, grimacing at the aching in his ribs and side. "If I go to the hospital, you have to promise me that you'll consider being my wife." Her mouth opened. Closed. Eyes widened. Head shook. "This isn't a proposal. You deserve something more romantic than this. But I need to know that you're just as serious about making this work as I am, pooh. We've wasted so much time, and since that was my fault, I have to make up for it. Will you make that promise to me?"

Riana remained silent for so long Luca began to question if now was the time to ask that of her. Just when he was about to lose hope, Riana smiled. She kissed his lips softly then kissed his nose with hers.

"I promise to take this just as seriously as you. Now let's wash you up so we can get to the hospital."

UNTITLED

"You should do what you wanna
You can do what you want 'cause
I'm gon' set you free, yeah
Visions of you leaving me, yeah
Next thing I know you're leaving me
No tellin' where you were leading me,
leading me
You're leaving me"

CHAPTER 22

 he past
Luca

AS SOON AS *Luca opened the door Riana fell into his arms.
He let out a sigh of relief at the feel of her warmth. It felt kind
of shady to be receiving so much peace and happiness having
her because of the situation he'd helped her and her family
out with, but Luca was taking every chance he could to see
and talk to Riana.*

*She'd cut him off two weeks ago. For two weeks straight,
she ignored his calls and text messages. If he popped up on
her, she'd ignore him. Luca had no clue how he was going to
make things right. Then, he was granted an opportunity to
show Riana just how much he cared about her.*

*Earlier today, her niece had gone missing. When her
sister, Candace, arrived at the daycare to pick her up she was*

informed that her daughter's father had picked her up. Seeing as they weren't on the best of terms, Candace assumed the worst. It didn't make it any better that Brandon wasn't answering her phone calls. Luca didn't know what their issue was, but he'd become aware that there was in fact an issue when he went to pick Riana up one day and saw them arguing.

Because Brandon was her father and on the list of people who could pick her up, the police weren't offering much help, so Riana took matters into her own hands to find her niece. She called Luca, knowing there wasn't too much of anything happening in the streets that he couldn't find out about. All Luca needed was his name, address, and the names of his parents or siblings, and he told her to leave the rest to him. About two hours passed before Luca found both Brandon and Sadie. He found them at the airport. Brandon had purchased them both one-way tickets to Chicago, where he planned to keep her until Candace got back with him.

Naturally, Riana had gone back home with Candace and Sadie, and Luca didn't expect to hear from her until tomorrow. But here she was. At his doorstep. Clinging to him as if her life depended on it. No. As if he was her life.

When Luca realized she wasn't going to let him go any time soon, he wrapped her legs around him and carried her into his home.

"Thank you," she whispered into his ear before kissing it as he sat them both down. "She would be gone if it weren't for you."

"It's nothing."

Riana's head shook as she ran her hands down the back of his. "Why'd you do that? You didn't have to do that. I've been ignoring you for..."

"It doesn't matter what happens between us, Santee, I will always come running when you call."

Her forehead went to his as she sniffled. "Why were you with her, Luca? Why would you do that to me?"

Luca sighed as he ran his hands down her back. It was time for him to be honest with her... and himself.

"Because I'm falling... because I love you, Riana." She lifted her forehead from his and looked into his eyes. "Because I'm in love with you."

Confusion covered her face. "That doesn't make sense."

Luca smiled softly. "It makes sense to me. I've avoided love all of my adult life. There was no desire within me for that shit. I didn't want to hurt a woman the way my mother hurt, and I wasn't trying to be trapped and have to settle down. I'm in the prime of my life, and I wanted to make the most of it. Having children or a woman at home waiting for me would slow me down. So I fucked around with her because I was trying to convince myself that I didn't love you. That I'd be straight without you. But being with her only made me want you more."

"Why didn't you come to me, Luca?"

"And say what, Riana?" Luca put her on the side of him and stood. "That I'm fucking with other females because I'm in love with you? How does that sound?"

"Unhealthy and toxic as hell." Riana smiled as she stood too. Her arms wrapped around him. "And it's all the more *reason for us not to be together. I don't want you to feel like you can't have your fun and live your life because of me."*

"I do want you, Riana. I just don't want commitment. I don't want you to have expectations and I disappoint you."

Riana released him and put some space between them. She covered her face and released a loud exhale before lowering her hands and confessing, "I love you too. Lord knows I tried to fight it because I knew I couldn't trust you, but I love you too."

"You can trust me. You can trust me to give you what I say I'm going to. You just can't expect anything more."

Turning her back to him, Riana flung her head back and chuckled.

"My mother will throw me out if she finds out I'm talking to you again. She said she refuses to watch me settle and end up like her and Candace."

"Then move in with me." Luca stepped in front of her. Lifting her head and her eyes to him by her chin. "This is your life to live, not hers. You know I'll do right by you just as long as you ride with me. Stay here, Riana. Let me love you the best way I know how."

He could see the war within her play out on her face. All Luca could do was pray she listened to her heart and not her mind. As selfish as it was, there was no part of him that wanted to let her go. And he was willing to do whatever it took to satisfy her and make her feel loved. Just... without the commitment. No one or nothing would take his freedom away from him. Especially something as fickle as love.

"Okay. I'll move in. But just for a few months, Luca. I'm

not going to be with you for more than a year without a commitment from you. After we hit one year, you commit, or we're done."

Luca smiled as he pulled her into his arms.

"Whatever you say, pooh."

UNTITLED

"How did we get away from love?
How did love get away from us?
Not my time, I should wait for love
Waste of time, what a waste of love
You're my wasted love, wasted love"

uca

LUCA WAS aware of the fact that something was bothering Riana, but she wasn't talking to him about it. David had called him earlier and said she was acting funny during their lunch yesterday, but Luca didn't think anything of it. It was one thing for her to be acting funny with him; it was something totally different when she started acting different with Luca.

They had breakfast with her mother and siblings. Things were a bit awkward in the beginning because it was the first time they'd seen them together in years. That changed after Luca made his intentions with Riana clear. Candace had been in his corner ever since he helped find

Sadie, so she was an easy win. Even Cameron couldn't help but respect the man Luca had become. Was becoming.

It was Rittany that was the hardest sell of them all. She made it clear that she trusted her daughters' judgment, and that only time would tell if he was really sincere this time around.

After breakfast, they went to church. Luca thought that would help pull Riana out of her funk, but it didn't. They stopped by his mother's house, where they spent time with her and Luca's siblings. Riana and Ladia's bond was so rich they were able to talk and laugh as if no time had passed since the last time they spoke. For a brief moment, Riana seemed happy and at peace, but as soon as they were alone again her funk returned.

Luca couldn't help but feel as if he was the cause of her sour mood, so when they made it back to her place he questioned her about it. She brushed him off, saying he was creating a problem where there wasn't one, so he let it go. He let it ride, giving her space. While she laid down, he lounged on the couch. Maybe she was just tired, Luca reasoned, trying to convince himself that there wasn't more.

She offered to cook dinner so they could stay in, but she was so deep in her thoughts that she burned the first batch of fish. Wanting to help lighten her mood, Luca FaceTimed Tatiana so she could see her, but she didn't. In fact, at the sound of Tatiana's voice on the phone, Riana locked herself in the bathroom and didn't come out until he'd disconnected the call.

And that was the final straw.

"What the fuck is wrong with you?" Luca questioned, following her from the bathroom to her bed. "And don't tell me nothing either. You're quiet and distant, burning food, then I call my daughter and you hide in the bathroom until I end the call. What's up with you?"

With a roll of her eyes, Riana pinched the bridge of her nose. As if he was irritating her. As if he'd been the one acting funny all day.

"It's nothing. Nothing that I want to talk to you about."

"What the hell is that supposed to mean? We keeping secrets from each other now?"

"We don't have to talk about everything, Luca."

"Since when? Even when I'm going through shit with Aaliyah or the business that doesn't concern you I still communicate with you so you won't think my fucked up mood is because of you. You can't give me that same respect?"

Her jaw clenched as her head shook. She chuckled quietly before running her fingers through her hair.

"Is this about me asking you to marry me? We've been seeing each other less ever since, and the first day we spend together this is how you act."

Riana stood. "I'm asking you to let it go."

She left her room. Normally Luca would have tried to stick around so they could work whatever the issue was out. Not this time around. Not when he had no idea what the problem was to begin with. That was fine. If Riana didn't want to talk about this, they didn't have to talk at all.

UNTITLED

"Broken hearts are made for two
One for me and one for you"

uca

HER ASS SHOOK. Vigorously. But the shaking mound of meat did nothing to sway Luca. Or stiffen his flaccid dick. There was nothing any woman in this club could offer him that topped the mere pleasure he received just by being in Riana's presence. No matter how much she irritated the fuck out of him, Luca belonged to her, and he was reminded of that truth right now.

Grabbing her waist, Luca stopped the woman's twerking. He sat her on the side of him, between him and David, then handed her a drink. It wasn't his intention to let another woman entertain him for the evening, but when David called him for a guy's night out Luca decided to make the most of it. He'd called Riana a couple of hours earlier to apologize for leaving without resolving their issue, and she ignored his call. Now, he found himself flirting just for the hell of it because he was bored.

Because he craved the attention.

Because he wanted to see if he still had it.

And by the way the woman was throwing herself at him, there was no question in Luca's mind that he did.

"What are you doing when you leave here?" she asked, gripping Luca's thigh.

"Going home to my woman." Luca moved her hand from his thigh. Had David not been there, he probably would have let her shoot her shot, but the last thing he needed was for him to nag him about being faithful or to tell Riana what had happened.

"Does she let you have company?"

Luca chuckled as he poured himself a glass of Moet.

"Nah. She stingy as hell. My pooh don't play that shit."

"Your pooh is here right now," David added, pointing towards Riana as she made her way over to them. "My fault, bro. She asked me where I was. I didn't think she was gon' pull up."

Luca sighed as he ran his hands over his fade. This was the last thing he needed. Things were already off between them, for reasons he still had no clue about, and now she was going to think he was out here cheating.

"You might want to leave," Luca suggested, staring at Riana as she made her way over to them.

"Why?"

"I'm about to head out," David declared, standing to his feet. He shook hands with Luca, shaking his head in the process. "Be humble. Don't have my best friend out here acting a fool."

"Then take her with you. Shit, she probably trying to talk and drink with you anyway."

David chuckled even though Luca was dead serious.

"Nah, my guy. I'll link up with her, but I'm done playing referee with y'all."

Luca couldn't even blame him. David had been in the middle of tons of arguments between the two years ago. Didn't really seem fair to put him in the middle of it now. Still, David had the type of loyalty that had him lingering around just to make sure Riana would be straight anyway. He hugged her and whispered something in her ear that caused her to nod before making his way over to the bar. Standing a foot away from them, Riana looked from Luca to... whoever her name was that was sitting next to him.

When she made it directly in front of Luca she asked, "What the fuck are you doing, Luca?"

"You ready to talk now? 'Cause when I called your ass earlier you ignored my phone calls."

"This your girl?" She looked at Riana. "Why you don't like to share? These niggas for everybody these days."

Riana chuckled as she looked at her briefly before turning her attention back to Luca.

"I wish I could argue with you but you right about that. These niggas *are* for everybody these days."

They had an intense stare down as the woman stood.

"If things don't work with her, look me up on IG. My name is..."

"Can you get any more disrespectful?" Riana asked, turning to face her. "Clearly you know who I am, so respect the code and gone about your business."

She chuckled and confessed, "Bitch, I don't owe you shit. Only female I'm loyal to is myself. If I want your man I'll take 'em, and if you're lucky, I'll send him back to you when I'm done."

Riana's eyes tightened as Luca stood.

"Alright, that's enough. I didn't mind playing around with you and having a lil' fun, but you taking it too far now."

Riana chuckled as Luca stepped between them, wrapping his arm around her from behind.

"You know what? I'm so sick of this shit, Luca. For real. You entertain these hoes and then wonder why they jock you. And I'm the one that ends up looking like a fool, because you're out here doing stupid shit."

"Who you calling a hoe?"

"Say one more thing to me and I'm going to break your fucking nose."

Now this, this was a side of Riana that Luca didn't see often. Back in the day, she was quiet and reserved, only pouncing when threatened or attacked. In fact, she went to war more over people bringing dishonor to the names and character of those she loved than she defended herself. The old Luca would have been turned on by her fire and willingness to throw down. The new Luca wanted to protect her at all costs – even if that meant protecting her from himself and the effects of dealing with him.

"Hoe, you ain't gon do shi—"

Her words were cut off by Riana's fist connecting with her mouth. Grabbing her by the front of her dress, Riana punched her in the nose twice before Luca could grab her and pull her away. As livid as Luca was, he couldn't help but be soothed by her calmness as he carried her out of the club.

"What was that, Santee? You fighting over something that's already yours these days?"

"No! I beat her ass because she disrespected me. I shouldn't have even had to do that had you not disrespected me first by even entertaining her. Let me the fuck go!" Riana wiggled to be free of his grip, but Luca didn't release her until they were at her car, and as soon as he did she smacked him. "I can't believe you! We have one little fight and you're looking to replace me already?"

"Mane, chill out. Wasn't nobody trying to replace you. Yea, I was flirting with her, but I told her I was going home to you. I didn't even get her name. We talked, and I bought her a couple of drinks but that's it."

Riana's facial expression relaxed as her shoulders loosened. Her head shook softly as she opened the door to her car.

"Now you don't have anything to say?"

"Just leave me alone, Luca."

It felt like déjà vu. Like the night they'd ended their unofficial relationship all over again. That night, seven years ago, Luca let her walk away without a fight. This time, that wouldn't be the case. He'd let it go for now, but he wouldn't rest until she came clean about what was bothering her, and he made her believe she wasn't the type of woman that could be replaced.

UNTITLED

"Tell me have you heard the news
We are now in love"

CHAPTER 25

The past
Riana

HER NERVES WERE GETTING the best of her. Luca would be out of the shower any minute now, and she couldn't hold on to this secret any longer. They'd been as careful as they possibly could be, even though she wasn't on birth control. Luca always pulled out. Except that one time...

Well, she thought he did. Couldn't say for sure. They both were drunk and not in their right minds. But that was how you brought the new year in, right? Drunk out of your mind making love to the one you love.

"Dammit, Riana," she whispered, pounding her palm against her forehead gently. "I can't be pregnant. Not right now."

But she was. The six pregnancy tests she'd taken earlier confirmed that.

The water cut off. Shower curtain slid back. He'd be out any minute now.

Riana stood and began to pace. Nibbling on her bottom lip, she looked at the door of Luca's bathroom. Deciding this wasn't the right time to tell him, Riana put on her clothes as quickly as she could. By the time she was fully dressed, Luca was coming out of the bathroom with only a towel wrapped around his waist. He looked from her face to the bag in her hand.

"Where you going?"

Swallowing hard, Riana leaned against the dresser. "Candace's house."

Luca nodded, slowly walking over to her. "How long will you be there? I thought tonight was movie night?"

"It." Riana cleared her throat, unknowingly putting space between them. "It is, but you got in pretty late, so I figured you might want to rest instead."

With a smile, Luca cupped her cheek and pulled her into his chest.

"I'm never too tired for you. I haven't had you all day, pooh. Give me my time with you."

Riana nodded, forcing a smile. Satisfied with her answer, Luca turned to head back to the bathroom, but his steps halted when she blurted, "I'm pregnant."

His body grew rigid as he took in a deep breath. When he released it, Luca turned to face her.

"What did you say?"

"I'm pregnant."

"How?"

Riana searched his eyes and his face for anger. Sadness. Happiness. Something. All he gave her was a stone face and a blank stare.

"New Year's Eve I guess. I'm just as surprised as you."

Bobbing his head, Luca ran his hands down his face. "Okay. Cool. Just let me know when you make the appointment to take care of this and I'll go with you."

He walked away, as if that was the end of the conversation. For a while, all Riana could do was stand there, staring at the space he once occupied. It wasn't until he came back out of the bathroom with his boxers on that Riana was able to speak.

"What do you mean take care of this?"

Luca's stone face temporarily covered with confusion, but he fixed it rather quickly.

"I told you I didn't want no kids. I assumed you'd want to get an abortion."

"An abortion?" Riana chuckled, putting her hands on her hips. "I am not getting rid of my baby, Luca. You should have thought about that before you came inside of me."

"No, your ass should have remembered what I said and got on some birth control. I ain't taking care of no kids, Riana."

"Then I'll take care of him or her myself," Riana decided, grabbing her bag and heading out of his room.

"Why? So you can go around telling folks I'm a deadbeat? Fuck outta here with that shit. Let me know when *you make the appointment and lock my door on your way out."*

Leaning against the wall, Riana cried quietly as she waited. Waited for him to come to his senses and come after her. To say to hell with this no commitment thing and make an honest woman out of her for the sake of their new family. But that didn't happen. Luca never came after her, and Riana was sure that she'd be done with him after this.

UNTITLED

"So I guess that I should mention
That I am in no condition
To put you in this position."

iana

THERE WAS no need for Riana to question who was at her door. It couldn't have been anyone but Luca. After what happened at the club, she blocked his number and put her phone on do not disturb just in case he tried to call from someone else's. When Riana first texted David, she was hoping to meet him, get a few drinks, then seek advice on what she should do with Luca.

The time for her to give Herbert Luca's heart on a platter was drawing nigh, and if she didn't produce, she'd be the one losing her life. Unintentionally, she began to distance herself from Luca. Said it was because he'd have to get used to living without her anyway. Somewhere along the lines he noticed, and the second he questioned her about it Riana went into defense mode.

It would have been easiest for her to call off their relationship, but was that even possible at this point? Now that she'd agreed to taking their reconnection just as seriously as he was? Hell, he wanted to marry her for God's sake. How crazy would she look if she randomly broke up with him?

No. It would have to be for a reason. She would have to get him to give up on her. But tonight, it looked as if the roles had been reversed. As if Luca had gone back to his old ways and given Riana the perfect out. No way would she spend the rest of her life with a cheater, no matter how short of a time span that was.

After putting her hair up in a ball, Riana headed to her front door. At any other time, she would have grabbed the pistol that was in the wooden basket that held her umbrellas, but she felt no need. It had to be Luca. Just had to.

Riana looked out of the peephole, and sure enough, Luca was on the other side. She opened the door wide enough for them to see each other, but it certainly wasn't enough for him to step inside.

"Can I come in?"

As much as Riana wanted to say yes, she shook her head no.

"You can't use other women to downplay how you feel about me, Luca."

"I know." His voice was just as soft as his eyes. "But I wasn't going to have sex with her, you have to believe me."

"That's what you said back then too. You said you weren't having sex with them, but you were!"

Trying not to go back to that headspace, Riana slammed the door in his face to compose herself. After taking in a few deep breaths, she opened the door, expecting him to be gone. But he was still there, waiting for her.

"I shouldn't have kept what's been going on from you," Riana admitted, "For that I apologize." Luca nodded. "But you can't go to a club and fuck around with someone else just because you don't get your way with me, Luca. That's not healthy."

"I know. I fucked up. That's all I can say. You're not going to believe me anyway."

"I thought you changed, but you're the same."

With a chuckle, Luca lifted his hands in prayer position. "If I was the same, I wouldn't be here. I'd be knee deep in another woman's pussy. But I'm trying to show you that I love you and want you and only you. That I've changed. What I won't do, is let you punish me for my past all over again. I'm sorry for flirting with her, but that's all it was. I didn't have sex with her, and I don't plan on having sex with her. Whether you believe me or not is on you."

Riana watched him walk away. Desperately she wanted to call out for him, but it was best this way. It was best if they went their own way. Because in two weeks, both of their lives were going to drastically change.

UNTITLED

"I might fuck this up."

CHAPTER 27

 uca

"I just don't know what to do."

Luca sat back in his seat and looked towards the sky. He'd heard somewhere that lies were like stars, they always came out. Seven years ago, he told the lie that he could happily live without Riana. In hardly no time, he realized that wasn't true. Pride kept him from righting his wrongs then. And when Tatiana came along, the love he had for her temporarily blinded him to his lack of Riana's love. But that didn't last long, because one source of love could never take the place of another.

It didn't matter how many children he had and loved,

how successful and rich he was, or how many hobbies he took up – nothing could dull his love for Riana Santee.

"What is your heart telling you to do?" David asked before lifting his glass of whisky to his mouth.

"To let her go. It's clear this ain't what she want. For so long, I put my needs and wants above hers. Can't say I love her if I don't put her first."

"What makes you think that's what she wants?"

"Shit, the way she pushed me away. For days she's been distant and trying to put space between us. Then when we're together we fight. And when I fuck up for the first time since this started she uses that as an excuse to let me go."

David sighed as he pulled his phone out of his pocket. "Ari will kill me if she knew I showed you this, but that's my sis, and I have to do what I think is best for her." He put in his password and went to his text thread before handing it to Luca. "I don't know what she has going on, but something's going on, Luca. Now is not the time for you to pull away."

Luca looked over the conversation David had with Riana via text.

Sis: I loved him before I even knew why. That night at the pool hall, I loved him then. David. I loved him them. It's the kind of connection you can't explain even if you tried.

Work it out then, sis. You know I wouldn't lie for him. He made it clear to her that he was in a relationship. Yea, he shouldn't have been flirting with her and buying her drinks, but that's all it was.

Sis: All it was? David. That's like cheating. I know it's not that serious to you men, and maybe it's not serious to other women, but that's cheating to me. He was forging a connection with another woman. And he didn't even check her when I showed up. Out of respect, he should have dismissed her when he saw me. I'm tired of having to prove my position in his life David.

Have you talked to him about this? If he doesn't understand how this makes you feel he's not going to stop doing it. It means nothing to him. But if he knows it hurts you I know he'll stop.

Sis: It's best this way anyway. Lord knows I don't want us to be over, but this is for the best. ... I love the both of you.

I know that, but what's going on with you? You good sis?

"She didn't text back. Did you call her?"

"I called her, but she didn't answer."

"It didn't even register to me that she would consider something like that cheating, but I guess that makes sense. If I'm building any type of connection with a woman outside of her, physically, mentally, or emotionally, she thinks I'm giving away what belongs to her. Why didn't she just say that shit?"

"Because she's just as proud and crazy as you. What

would she say, Luca? I don't like when you entertain other women because it makes me feel like you're cheating? What would your response be?"

Luca remained silent as he massaged his temples. Realistically, he wouldn't have taken her concern seriously. All he would have done was try to make her see things his way instead of trying to understand her point of view. But there was something about being on the outside looking in, something about seeing her express herself to someone else, it was a blessing that felt like a violation at the same time. Luca was glad, however, that David gave him that glimpse into her mind.

"I need to go fix this shit with my baby."

Luca stood and shook David's hand before leaving. After sleeping on it, he was going to try his hardest to let her go again. Be satisfied with the small amount of time he'd had her for this time around. But now? There was no way he was letting Riana go. Especially over something as simple as this.

Not without a fight.

UNTITLED

"But whatever the case
You're my favorite mistake.
More than happy to make you."

CHAPTER 28

*he past*
Luca

HE'D TOLD himself that this wouldn't hurt. That there was no way in hell he could be attached to a baby that had been in Riana's womb for only six weeks. That there was no way in hell he could love a baby he'd never even met. But it did hurt. Hurt like hell. The second it was over, and Riana came out of the room, crashing into his arms as she sobbed, Luca's heart broke too.

Broke in two.

One piece for Riana. One piece for their unborn child. The child they'd never get to meet. Because of his mother. And his father. And his siblings' fathers. And their generational curse. And his lack of a desire to carry it on. But... it seemed... he'd started something even worse. Why, at least he and his siblings had life – even if their fathers weren't in it.

But his baby?

His baby was gone.

Luca looked over at Riana's now empty stomach, and he was no longer able to contain his tears.

"You need to get out. I gotta go."

Riana looked over at him, touching him gently at the sight of his tears.

"Please don't leave, Luca. I need you right now, and it's clear that you need me too."

"I need you to get out, so I can go."

Luca wiped his face, anger turning into shame during his moment of weakness. Riana stared at the side of his face, tears streaming down hers. She opened the door and got out, but before she closed it she asked, "Will you be gone long, Luca? I..." Her voice cracked, causing Luca to squeeze his eyes shut as more tears fell. "I can't take being alone right now."

"And I can't take being around you right now. That shit... it wasn't supposed to hurt like this, Santee!" Her head lowered as she cried harder, and it took everything within Luca to not console her. "The more I look at you... at your stomach... this was my fault, Riana. Our baby is gone because of me. I need some space, pooh. Please."

"Fine." Her voice grew cold as she wiped her face and added, "Take all the time you need."

Riana slammed the door and briskly walked towards

their home. Luca waited until she was inside to call David.
When he answered, Luca pulled out of his driveway.

"What's up?"

"Where you at, D? I need a few drinks."

UNTITLED

*"If you decide to stay
know there is no escape."*

CHAPTER 29

 iana

RIANA RUBBED sweaty palms against each other as she waited for Herbert. Her leg shook rapidly as she rolled her neck. She should have never agreed to this in the first place, but that's what anger and bitterness did to you. It made you care nothing about nothing but your pain and what it took to ease it. But love? Love made you selfless. Made you want to do whatever it took to protect the people who made you feel loved.

And that's exactly what Riana was about to do.

"I can't talk right now, beauty. Walk me to my car and make this quick."

Riana stood and began to walk down the hall with Herbert.

"This won't take long. I just came to tell you that I can't do this anymore."

Herbert stopped mid stride. He turned to face her, giving her a small smile before proceeding to walk down the hall.

"You don't get to quit, Riana. That's not how this business works."

Twisting her body slightly, Riana squeezed between two guards as she continued to follow Herbert into the living room.

"I understand that. I understand that I signed a contract. I'm more than prepared to give you your money back."

He stopped again, chuckling with a shake of his head as he grabbed his hat off the couch.

"Money I can do without. I have more of it than I can count. What I don't have is Luca Kareem added to my body count. It's your responsibility to take care of that for me."

She remained silent as they left the living room, trying to come to grips with what she was about to say. Do. The sacrifice she had to make. Riana waited until they were at Herbert's car to speak.

"It's a life for a life, right?" Herbert nodded, getting inside of the car after his guard opened the door. "Then I offer my life in exchange for his. You can kill me right now if that's what it takes to keep him safe."

Herbert's laugh infuriated Riana, but she kept her composure. Not only had she been stripped of her pistol at the door, but there was a hell of a lot of firepower aimed at her as they spoke. If there was one thing she could say about Herbert, it was that he was willing to pay any amount of money to keep him and the rest of his family safe, and his bodyguards had strict orders to kill anyone that posed a threat – male or female, friend or foe.

"You have twenty-four hours to change your mind. I want Luca here. At five P.M. Or you will take his place."

Riana stepped back and allowed his guard to close the door. She watched as his chauffeur drove off, then she went back to his house to retrieve her pistol. On her way out, Riana groaned at the sight of David.

"The hell is he doing here?" she asked herself, walking over to him.

"The hell you doing here?" David asked, pulling her into him for a side hug.

"I need to be asking you the same thing."

"Yea, well I asked first. What are you doing here?"

Riana licked the side of her mouth before shutting it and nibbling on her bottom lip. She'd held this secret for so long that it didn't feel right telling anyone about it. Not even her best friend. Then again, she'd held this secret for so long she was desperate to telling anyone about it. Who better than her best friend?

"I'm the Femme Fatale."

David's head shook as he took a step backwards. "No. You. No. Riana."

Riana pulled her bottom lip down and showed David the emblem that Herbert branded her with. Everyone on his team was required to get a brand to show their loyalty. Even with Riana's street identity being a secret, she was no different. There was a branded tiger hidden from the world on her bottom lip.

"The fuck, sis? Why?" David grabbed her by her jaw and pulled her closer, looking the brand over closely. "Does Luca know about this? He can't know about this."

At the mention of Luca's name, reality set in for David.

"David..."

"So you're the one Herbert hired to kill him? And you agreed? Now that's some cold-blooded shit."

David turned, heading for his car.

"David, wait. Let me explain." She grabbed his arm trying to stop him, but he continued.

"I'm not the one you owe an explanation; Luca is. I want to ask you about this shit and what would possess you to work for him or anyone else in this capacity, but that's not even important to me right now. He needs to know."

"Will you stop walking and talk to me?" Riana stepped in front of David, hoping he wouldn't trample her to get to his car. "It's a long story, one that I don't feel like getting into, but all you need to know right now is that I am not going to kill Luca. Yes, that's the reason I positioned myself in his life again, but that's not my M.O. I fell in love with him all over again, and I'm going to do whatever it takes to keep him safe."

David stared into her eyes, as if he was still unable to believe what she was saying.

"Herbert swears by a life for a life, Riana. If you don't give him Luca..."

Riana's head hung. She gave him a slight nod.

"I'm taking care of it, D."

"No. This is bullshit."

David continued towards his car.

"Don't tell him. He doesn't need to know."

"Do you hear yourself right now, Ari? That mane will kill you, and then he'll turn around and pay someone else to kill him. If he doesn't give a fuck about his own son, what the hell makes you think he's going to spare you?"

David's countenance dropped as soon as he realized what he'd said. He opened the door to his car, but Riana shut it quickly.

"What do you mean if he doesn't give a fuck about his son? That's what this is all about. He's trying to avenge his son's death, and the fact that his other son is in jail."

Shaking his head, David looked around the mansion.

"Get in the car," he ordered as he got inside.

Riana scurried to the other side of the car. David opened her door from the inside, and she quickly got in.

"Tell me what you were doing here, David."

David massaged his chin in that same way Luca did, and she couldn't help but miss him already.

"Herbert is Luca's father."

"That doesn't make sense." Riana's head shook as she turned in her seat towards him. "Harry is Luca's father. And Raymond is his uncle. They're the reason this war is still going on. Herbert thinks one of them killed his son, and because they left town, he seeks revenge by killing Luca."

"That's not the whole truth. Herbert pursued Lucy,

Luca's mother, at the same time as Harry. He didn't even want her, just wanted her to avoid Harry having her. She thought Harry was Luca's father, but it's actually Herbert. In an attempt to keep Luca safe, she allowed both Harry and Herbert to believe that Harry was Luca's father. A few years passed before Harry found out, and when he did, he went after Herbert for sleeping with his woman. It was a wrong place at the wrong time kind of thing. Instead of the bullet hitting Herbert it hit his son. Harry knew there was no coming back from that, so he and Raymond left. That's why he never tried to maintain a relationship with Luca. He didn't see the need since he wasn't his son."

"How do you know this? Does Herbert know? How could he want to kill his own son?"

David's eyebrows wrinkled, as if rehashing the story was giving him a headache.

"I know because when I went to see Luca one day, Herbert was there. He was having a heated discussion with Lucy, and when it was over, she was sobbing. I guess she was so distraught that she felt like she had to talk to somebody, and since I was there, she picked me.

As soon as Harry left town, she told Herbert the truth. She hoped knowing Luca was her son would keep him from continuing on with the beef, but it didn't. It paused it for a while but that's it. The nigga refused to even acknowledge the fact that Luca was his son. But, he did pull up on me one day, trying to see what I knew. He made me promise not to tell Luca that he was his father.

Of course I didn't agree." David paused, and Riana 's

head shook in disbelief. "But he... made me an offer that I couldn't refuse. In exchange for my silence, he's been giving me ten thousand dollars a month. If I ever tell Luca the truth, the money stops and so does my heart."

David took her hand into his, pulling her back into the moment.

"It's been eating at me to keep this secret, but I felt like it was best if he never knew the truth. Herbert doesn't give a fuck about him. He has plenty of children out here, but if he didn't raise them in this house, he doesn't claim them. Herbert is a heartless bastard, and it messes with me to know he was able to turn you into one too."

Riana jerked her hand away from his and had to keep herself from slapping him.

"How dare you talk to me that way, like you haven't been paid to keep this secret from your own best friend!"

"Every dime he gives me I give to Luca! I put that money into a bank account that he doesn't even know about. Should anything happen to him or Aaliyah every dime of it goes to Tatiana. And if he can retire and go legit, it will go to him. He will never be able to question my loyalty, but clearly he can't say the same about you."

Silence fell. Neither of them spoke a word for what felt like an eternity. She hated to admit it, but what David had said was true. All of it. It was for the best if Luca didn't know Herbert was his father. How could he live with knowing his own father wanted him dead? And Herbert *had* turned her into a heartless beast. But that was only with her permission. After Luca had taken her heart, Riana didn't give a damn what became of her.

Herbert preyed on her during her weakest moment, and as much as she wanted to blame it on Luca and Herbert, this was the first time in a really long time that Riana took responsibility for it herself.

"You're right, Luca would have every right to question my loyalty. I shouldn't have taken the job to begin with. You don't understand what it's been like for me, David. Blaming him for my pain was the only way I could keep myself from taking responsibility and going crazy over the terrible decisions I made.

I chose to be with a man who didn't value me enough to commit to me. I chose to not get on birth control. I chose to have an abortion."

"Ari..."

"I chose to leave that night. I chose to go to that shelter. I chose to trust Herbert after he saved me. I chose to let him mold me into who he wanted me to be, because I was tired of being myself."

"I'm sorry, okay? It's not all on you. We all played a part in this. Me too. If I would have been there for you that night, or even tried to find you more afterwards, maybe I could have kept you from him."

Seeing no need to go back and forth with him over this, Riana opened the door.

"Give me your word that you won't tell him who I am. You have to believe me when I say I'm not going to try to kill him. I don't have it in me. If I've learned anything since I've been back home, it's that I'm not as cold and heartless as I thought I was."

Riana stepped out of the car, but she didn't close the door behind her. She wouldn't leave until he gave her his word.

"You have twenty-four hours to tell Luca the truth. If you don't, I'm doing it for you."

UNTITLED

"There's no one here to save you.
But you're so brave, stone cold crazy for
loving me
Yeah, I'm amazed, I hope you make it out alive"

CHAPTER 30

 he past
Riana

"RIANA..."

"You promised!" Luca grabbed her wrist as soon as her hand shoved his chest. "You said a heart for a heart! I gave you mine, but I've never had yours. Have I?"

Her sadness was beginning to be replaced with anger, causing her to swing at Luca's face with her free hand. Grabbing her wrist, Luca pulled both of her arms behind her and pressed her body into her car. Resting his forehead on hers, Luca exhaled deeply, and as Riana inhaled his exhale, his calmness entered her. He held her there until her breathing slowed down.

"You're the only woman that's ever had access to my heart. I promise you that. But I don't want to settle down right now, Riana, and you deserve better than that." Luca kissed her lips softly. "Than this." He brushed her nose with his gently. "Than me." Releasing her wrists, Luca took Riana's face into his palms by her cheeks, forcing her to look into his eyes. "I'm a motherfucker, that I know. I can't keep hurting you, Riana. Let me go, pooh."

Her eyebrows wrinkled as her eyes squeezed shut. Clawing at his hands, Riana tried to push them from her face, but Luca held on.

"Riana, look at me."

"Just let me go, Luca. You want me to let you go, you're free of me."

A few seconds passed before Luca released her. He'd cut her so deep it was hard to breathe. To stand. Her body grew weak. Sliding down against the car, Riana covered her face, finally allowing her tears to fall freely. Unsure of how much time had passed, Riana weakened even more when she felt arms wrap around her.

There was no need for her to look and see who it was. Those arms enclosed around her and comforted her many nights over the years.

"I'm so sorry," David whispered, lifting Riana to her feet. "I tried to get him not to go out tonight, Ari, but this was his way of dealing with it. I told him that y'all needed to heal together but this was easier for him."

Riana remained silent as she held on to David. Her tears continued to stream down her cheeks. And they weren't just over Luca. They were over the life that was no longer inside of her too.

If Luca wanted to leave, she'd let him, but there was no mistaking it – he'd taken her heart with him too.

The entire time Riana drove home she felt as if she was on auto pilot. So much so that she silently thanked God for getting her there safely as she stepped out of her car. Her eyes were just as clouded with tears as her mind was clouded with thoughts of Luca. And their baby. And the mess that she'd become over the past year. And what she was going to do now that they were over.

She couldn't possibly go back home. No. Her pride wouldn't allow that. Rittany had warned her that this was what would happen. Riana wouldn't dare let her know she was right.

Riana went inside of her home, of Luca's home, and packed all of her things. With no idea of where she was about to go, she was in absolutely no rush at all. There was no way she could go to any of her friends. No. They all looked up to Riana and admired her relationship with Luca. How were they going to react when they knew the truth?

"I'm such a fool," she whispered, wiping her face of more tears.

The sound of the door opening and closing caught Riana off guard. As far as she knew, Luca wouldn't be coming home any time soon."

Quickly grabbing her bags, Riana hoped they wouldn't fight again before she left. All she wanted to do was leave peaceably and figure out what to do with herself. While she went down the stairs, Luca came up. They stopped in the middle. Unable to take him peering down at her, Riana mumbled, "I'm leaving, and you won't ever have to see me again."

She tried to walk around him, but Luca's hand on her shoulder stopped her.

"Where are you going to go?"

Riana smiled before licking her lips. Not wanting to tell him she'd probably end up at a shelter or sleeping in her car, she told him, "Cameron's place. Or Candace."

"Well, if you want to get your own spot, there's more than enough money in the account I opened for..."

"The card and checkbook are on the dresser. I don't need your money, and I don't want anything else to do with you."

She continued down the stairs with him following behind.

"Can I at least help you with your bags?"

Her head shook as she fought to compose herself. "No. I got it." But she didn't have it. After taking three more steps, she stumbled over the one of the bags, dropping the rest and almost tumbling down the steps – if Luca wouldn't have grabbed her.

For a moment, she allowed herself to relish in the relief of being in his arms. But that faded away quickly when he said, "Riana, I'm sor–"

"No," she roared, pushing him off of her. "Save your apologies. I'm tired of your apologies. They mean nothing to me."

Luca released her and watched as she jogged down the stairs to collect her things.

"You don't have to go. You can stay here until you find a

place," Luca offered, but that was a set up. There was no way she could be in his presence and not fall for him all over again. Not forgive him for hurting her all over again. Not convince herself that being with him was better than being alone all over again.

No.

This cycle had to end.

Now.

UNTITLED

"Please don't take my hand if you don't plan to
Take a stand and me a man who
Understands that I'm no walk in the park
All these scars on my heart"

iana

"THANK YOU FOR COMING," was Riana's greeting.

"Thank you for calling," was Luca's.

She stepped to the side so he could enter, eyes lowering at the bags that were in his hands. After talking to David, it was even more clear what Riana had to do. No matter what happened between them over the years, Riana could never question Luca's love. There may have been times where he struggled with showing it or didn't show it at all because of self-preservation, but Riana could never question his love. And he would never be able to question hers.

But loyalty.

That was a different story.

In the past, Luca was more loyal to himself than her.

And this time around, Riana was dead set on being more loyal to herself than him.

That wasn't the case, though.

It was impossible to not do anything but give her relationship with Luca her all at this point. He was too caring, too present, too loyal, too loving, and far too giving to receive anything less than her love and loyalty in return.

Though her intentions may have been impure when she first returned to his life, there was nothing Riana wanted to do more than take care of him. And Tatiana.

Her plan was to cook him a good meal, get him full, fuck him long, then put him to bed. When he awoke tomorrow morning, it would be to a letter that explained everything. All Riana could do was pray that he forgave her and didn't harbor too much hate against her for temporarily agreeing to bring him harm.

"You haven't started cooking yet have you?"

"No, not yet." She'd had the idea to call him on her way home and hadn't had time to do much of anything before he arrived. "Why?"

Luca handed her the bags. "Get dressed. I'm taking you out."

Looking down at the bags, Riana was unable to take them right away. "You didn't have to get me anything, and we don't have to go out, Luca..."

"I'd already purchased these things for you. Just had to wait for them to be delivered. And I want us to go out. We have a lot to talk about, Riana, and I want this night to be special no matter how that conversation ends."

She couldn't help but wonder if David had spilled the beans already, but he couldn't have. Luca wouldn't have been so calm if he did. Riana gave him a slight nod before heading for her room. With each step her excitement grew. Like a kid on Christmas, she opened the bags one by one. They all came from her favorite place – Lilac Shade.

The first bag had a pair of wine red Becca pumps inside. The second bag had a gorgeous, black lace bra and panty set. The third bag had a ruffled, one shoulder, sleeveless wine red dress. With a v neck cut, Riana was sure it would show the perfect amount of cleavage. Putting it up to her, Riana smiled at the length. It was knee length with a wide mid-thigh split.

Luca knew her style well.

Showering as quickly as she possibly could, Riana put on Luca's favorite lotion and perfume to smell on her. She made her face up lightly and put big, loose flowing curls in her hair. Once dressed, she headed for the living room to gain his approval – hoping the outfit looked as good on her as he imagined it would.

Luca looked up when she entered, smiling widely at the sight of her. He stood, eyes taking in every inch of her.

"Can we stay in?" he asked as he walked in her direction. "I can feast on you all night and be full."

Riana practically melted in his arms when they wrapped around her. His nose inhaled her scent before he placed a kiss to her neck.

"And you put on my favorite perfume too. You tryna get pregnant tonight?"

She giggled as he turned her in his arms, but her life ending in less than twenty hours wiped the smile off her face.

"I'm glad you like it. You did a very good job picking this dress."

Luca lowered himself to peck her lips quickly. Gently. And Riana couldn't help but wonder why he was holding back. Deciding not to question it, Riana followed his lead out of the living room. His hand enveloped hers, and she tried to implant that feeling, this moment, into her memory. It would be the only thing that carried her through when she went back to Herbert.

The ride was relaxed. On the way to the restaurant they made small talk. Each other's days, what shows they'd been watching together, and Tatiana were topics of conversation.

When they made it to the restaurant, they both spent a great deal of the first few minutes avoiding each other's eyes. Every time they'd lock, they would smile and share a quiet laugh.

"Truth?" Luca spoke breaking the silence.

"Truth."

At this point, nothing else would do. The ambiance was beautiful. They were in a darkened corner of the restaurant, their view illuminated by candles and the night sky through the wall to floor length mirror. Soft music was provided by a live band in the background. And bubbling champagne fizzed in their cups, just as live and full of energy as Riana's heart was.

"When you first came back into my life, I thought you

were setting me up. Thought Herbert sent you. There was talk of you being seen with him a while back, but I didn't believe it." Riana's heart dropped as Luca sat up in his seat. "When you would sleep, I would search every part of your body for his brand, and when I didn't find it I'd feel like shit. I knew I could easily find it on your body and know the truth, but a part of me refused to believe it was you. So I struggled with accepting that you were the Femme Fatale and accepting that you were gracious enough to give me a second chance after everything I'd put you through. Neither seemed real."

Riana blinked a few times and swallowed hard. Hands in her lap, she twiddled her thumbs and tried her hardest not to let him know anything either way.

"What do you think about me now?"

"Sometimes I think I know you better than anyone else in the world. Sometimes I don't think I know you at all." He leaned in. Voice lowered. "But I want to know you. I want to get to know you all over again, Santee. All I can do is pray that whatever you're going through right now won't keep you from letting me."

Riana drummed her thighs as she smiled softly. This seemed like the worst time and perfect time to tell him the truth, and she had no clue what to do. Her eyes sealed tightly, and when they opened she whispered, "You were right."

Tears blurred her eyes, but she refused to let them fall. She'd gotten herself into this mess, and she would be a G no matter what it took to get out.

"About what?"

Her pointing and thumb finger went to her bottom lip. Eyes closed, Riana pulled her lip down so he could see the brand. She let a few seconds pass before closing her mouth and opening her eyes. For a few seconds, Riana remained quiet and waited for a response. When he gave her that same stone expression and empty eyes she spoke.

"He groomed me. And I can't lie, it felt good using and hurting men. I was bitter and broken over what I'd experienced with you." She paused as he downed his glass of champagne. "I came back home, and my grandmother's wish on her birthday was for me to come back, settle down, and live a normal life. I agreed, and when I met up with Herbert he asked me to do one more hit for him. At first, I said no. But I was reminded of the pain and..." Her breathing was shaky as she exhaled. "I gave in. But, it took no time for me to realize I couldn't do that to you. No matter what we'd gone through I couldn't hurt you. And I couldn't take you from Tati."

"Is that why you started pushing me away?"

She nodded, watching him pour himself another glass of champagne.

"Yes. I knew Herbert would want a life for a life, and since I wouldn't give him yours he would want mine. We met earlier today. I have less than twenty-four hours to change my mind or he's taking me instead. And I'm not changing my mind."

"That's why you called me over?"

She nodded again. "Yes. I... wanted us to have one last

good night. I wanted to let you know that I forgive you for everything. And... I was going to write you a letter and pray that you forgave me too."

Luca stared at her until she looked away. It was torture waiting for him to say something. Anything. But she wouldn't dare rush his response.

"I want to be mad at you, but I can't because none of this would have happened had I not done what I did to you."

"No." Riana argued, voice low and crisp. "This was all me. My reaction was extreme..." Her head shook as she successfully fought back her second round of tears. "Because my love for you was. But that's no excuse. It doesn't justify what I agreed to do. You have my word, though, I mean you no harm."

Riana struggled with if she wanted to tell Luca the truth about his father or not. Unlike David, she didn't want to spill his secret. If Luca found out, it would be because David told him, and she prayed he never did. Had anything happened to her, Luca would go on a rampage, and it would kill him to know he'd killed his father.

"What time are you meeting with Herbert tomorrow?"

"Five."

Luca knocked back the rest of his champagne. He stood, pulling his wallet out and tossing a few bills onto the table. He walked over to her and placed a kiss to her forehead. Her nose. Her lips.

"I will take care of this." Her mouth opened but he

covered it with his finger. "And when I do, we will be even. Heart for a heart, right? I broke yours, you just broke mine."

He walked away, and suddenly, the perfect ambiance for love became the perfect ambiance for loneliness and heartbreak.

UNTITLED

"It's so dark yeah
But if you're a warrior, there's nothing to fear
Nothing to fear"

uca

"Are you okay, Daddy? You look sad."

Luca smiled with one side of his mouth. His eyes lifted towards Herbert's mansion briefly before he gave his attention back to Tatiana.

"I'm good, Tati. Daddy just wanted to see you before I took care of a little business."

Truth of the matter was, Luca had no idea how things were about to play out. Who knew if his plan would work when you dealt with someone as crazy as Herbert. Even with what Luca had, there was no telling how Herbert would respond.

"Where's my fairy? Can she come and pick me up with you this weekend?"

God.

Luca was hoping she wouldn't ask about Riana. Or him picking her up this weekend for that matter.

"I'm not sure, baby, but I'll see what I can do, okay? I'll call you before bedtime. I love you."

"Okay, Daddy. I love you too."

Tatiana handed Aaliyah the phone. They didn't talk about many things outside of Tatiana, but even she felt the need to ask, "You good?"

"Yea. Take care of my baby, alright?"

"Always."

Luca disconnected the call. He shot a quick I love you, to the group chat he had with his mother and siblings, then got out of his car. As soon as he did, the sound of guns being cocked rang all around him. Slowly, Luca made his way to Herbert's front door.

"What do you want?" the guard at the door asked.

"I need to see Herbert."

He made a quick call inside then searched Luca before letting him enter. Luca was led down the hall, and the house was dead silent. He reasoned within himself that this couldn't have been where Herbert was holding Riana, because if it was, there would be some type of commotion. A part of him prayed she was there. That she'd truly planned to sacrifice her life for his. Because that would be the only way he wouldn't feel like a fucking fool to think they could have had a future together.

The other part of him hoped she'd drained her bank accounts and made a run for it. Herbert may have looked for her for a while, but eventually he would have found another target and moved on.

Luca was led to an underground chamber, and the sight of Riana cuffed and gagged on her knees made him weak to his. There were six men surrounding her with guns pointed as Herbert sat and watched.

"Ah. Here he is. I knew he'd come to save you."

Riana lifted her head, and as soon as she saw Luca she shook her head as her eyes widened. This may not have been what she wanted, but this was how it had to be. Luca tried to walk over to Herbert, but his guards stopped him.

"I just want to give him this."

Luca lifted the manila envelope in his hand. The guard that was closest to Luca took it and handed it to Herbert. As he looked it over, Luca clarified what it was.

"That's an order of clemency for your son. He will be released from prison in thirty days, but that's only if both me and Riana make it out of here safely and Governor Eddington hears from me."

Herbert smiled. Then it dropped. Then he laughed. Once it died down he asked, "How in the hell did you pull this off?"

"That's none of your concern. If you need proof that that's official, Eddington's personal number is attached. Get my girl off her knees. *Now*."

With a gesture of his head, Herbert's men were lifting

Riana off the ground and removing the handcuffs and tape from across her mouth.

"The deal was a life for a life, right?" Luca continued, to which Herbert nodded. "I'm giving you your son back. That's more than enough for you to leave her alone. Are we on the same page?"

Herbert looked from Luca to Riana. His head shook as his mouth twisted up.

"I will spare both your lives. For now. But if a need arises, Riana is still indebted to me. This clears you, not her."

"But she came here to sacrifice herself for me. This covers her too."

Running his hand down his neck, Herbert chuckled as Riana made her way over to Luca.

"Riana." She turned to face Herbert. "When you join the prey, you *become* the prey. Goodbye for now, beauty."

Riana took a step towards Herbert, but before she could reply Luca's arm was wrapping around her and he pulled her away. He waited until they were outside to ask her, "Are you okay?"

She nodded, avoiding his eyes. At his car, Luca turned her towards him. "Let me look at you."

Taking her face into the palms of his hands, Luca looked her over attentively. "Did he hurt you?"

Her head shook. "What's wrong? Why can't you talk to me?"

"You weren't supposed to be here. I told you I was going to take care of this."

Luca smiled softly as he opened the passenger side door of his car. He helped her inside and took one last look at Herbert's mansion before getting in. For some reason, this didn't feel like the end. It may have been for now, but Luca was confident he'd hear from Herbert again.

"What did you have to do to get that clemency, Luca?"

He waited until they were headed down the road to answer her. "I had to give the Governor my word that I would stop dealing in his city. His state. I've basically been banished. He's given me thirty days to shut everything down and leave."

"What? No. I'm so sorry, Luca."

His hand went to her thigh and he squeezed it gently.

"It's cool. Maybe this is a sign that it was time for me to retire anyway."

"So what are you going to do now?"

"Move to South Carolina so I can be closer to Tati. Enroll in school like I always wanted to do. Start a new life. A legit life."

Riana covered his hand with hers. They rode in silence for a while, until Riana asked, "Why did you come for me?"

Luca thought over her question. He'd risked a lot to save her. His life could have been taken, and his daughter would be without a father. Was Riana worth the risk?

Hell yea.

"Because I love you, Riana Santee."

He saw her smile out of the corner of his eye.

"I love you too, Luca Kareem. But I just think... this

started on a lie. On a plot of revenge. And bitterness. And...
I don't think anything between us could work."

As much as Luca wanted to disagree, he couldn't.
They'd been through a lot. Everything they'd built up until
this point was built on a lie. It wouldn't stand, no matter
how hard the both of them tried.

"I agree."

Riana looked over at him, and Luca gave her his eyes.
He winked at her, and she smiled bitterly, failing horribly at
hiding the sadness that consumed her.

UNTITLED

*"'Cause you're so brave, stone cold crazy for
loving me
Yeah, I'm amazed, I hope you make it out alive"*

iana

RIANA STARED at the red door, unsure of what she was even doing there. She hadn't spoken to Luca in a month. Last time she saw him, they made love until the sun came up before saying their goodbyes. The next day, Riana made up in her mind to let him go and move on with her life. But her grandmother didn't plan on letting her get away with it that easily.

"I don't even know what I'm doing here, Grandma. What if he doesn't want to see me?"

"But what if he does?"

Massaging the back of her neck, Riana closed her eyes and sighed.

"If he wanted to be with me, I would have heard from him by now."

"You made me a deal, Ari. You promised me that you would come home, settle down, and live a normal life. How are you going to settle down and live a normal life if the man for you is hundreds of miles away?"

For about a week, Riana lived with a façade. She went on with her day to day life, as if nothing that happened for the past few months had happened. Most of her days were filled with work and her nights with partying to numb the pain of losing Luca all over again. And Tatiana.

It was during a conversation with her grandmother that Riana broke down and confessed how she really felt. That seemed to be the best decision Riana had made for a while, because her grandmother spent the next two weeks teaching her how to self-soothe and feel. Not just feel but feel better about herself and her life. Her grandmother used each of her senses to teach Riana about distress tolerance – skills used when it is impossible or difficult to change a situation and help with coping with pain.

The practice may have been a long time coming, a little over seven years to be exact, but it helped Riana not only deal with the pain of losing love now but the pain of losing her baby years ago as well.

After freeing up so much space in her heart and mind that was once consumed by pain, what Riana wanted was made clear – to live life with and love Luca Kareem.

But there was just one problem, Luca had just moved to South Carolina, and the fact that he didn't even say goodbye before he left led Riana to believe he didn't want to have anything to do with her.

"I know, Grandma, but..."

"No buts. There is no fear in love. Be confident in yourself and what you have to offer for once and go get your man."

"Yes, ma'am," Riana agreed through her smile.

She disconnected the call and stared at the red door once more. Finally willing herself to get out, Riana hesitantly walked to the door. After closing her eyes and inhaling three deep breaths, Riana knocked.

And waited.

And knocked some more.

And waited.

And knocked some more.

And waited.

Convinced he wasn't home, Riana called David to make sure he'd given her the right address. When he confirmed she was at the right place, Riana FaceTimed Luca. As soon as he answered and she saw his face, Riana couldn't help but smile.

"Hey," he greeted, smiling himself.

"Hi."

Luca's face scrunched up as he took in her background.

"Where are you?"

"I'm... at... your place. Where are you?"

He chuckled, then flipped the camera so she could see her front door.

"I'm at your place."

Walking to her car, Riana's head shook in disbelief.

"What are you doing there, Luca? If Eddington finds out..."

"I've got that under control." His smile faded slowly as he stared at her, and it was then that Riana felt the full essence of his absence from her life. "I couldn't get settled in Carolina or anywhere else without you."

"Me too!" Tatiana added in the background, as if she knew exactly what they were talking about.

"Tati says her too," Luca added through his chuckle.

"You came for me?"

"Of course. I told you I wasn't letting you go this time around."

"But, when we were leaving Herbert's house you agreed..."

"I agreed that what we had this time around started out on a lie, but I also told you that I wanted to get to know you all over again. Did I not?"

Riana nodded as she opened the door and got back inside of her car.

"Yes, but, I didn't think that would matter after you found out the truth."

"The only thing that matters to me is the love me and my daughter have for you. Now I'm willing to give us a genuine chance, Santee, but only if you are."

Her head bobbed rapidly as her eyes watered.

"That's all I want," she confessed as her tears began to fall. "Heart for a heart."

"Heart for a heart. Now dry them eyes, pooh. I'll text you Aaliyah's address. Wait there. I'm coming to get you."

"Okay," Riana agreed, then disconnected the call.

Resting her head on the headrest, Riana closed her eyes and smiled. This wasn't the turn she thought her life would make, but it was the outcome she most definitely needed.

Luca had come into her life like a thief in the night.

Stealing her heart and replacing it with his.

When he left, Riana swore she'd be empty for the rest of her life. But now that Luca had returned, he'd given her his heart back... and so much more.

THE END
FOR NOW
KEEP SWIPING :)

AFTERWORD

Be on the lookout for the next book, as this is literally the calm before the storm for Luca Kareem and Riana Santee. If you want, you can stop reading now and accept this as Riana and Luca's happily ever after. But for those of you who want to go a little deeper, I decided to add a second book literally the day before this one was supposed to go live, lol.

An old friend will be paying them a visit in South Carolina, and when he does, things will NEVER be the same again. To be the first to know when the second book in this standalone series drops, join my mailing list HERE or text AUTHORBLOVE to 22828.

P.S. Yes, you may have questions, such as when/if Luca will find out who his father is, if David is really a loyal friend, when you will get to see the MEAT of their relationship and how they grow and unfold for each other, and more, BUT remember, this is NOT over. All questions will be answered soon.

Write for you soon,
   B. Love

Just Love Me

A Hustler's Heaven In Hiding

ABOUT THE AUTHOR

Voted AAMBC's 2018 Romance author of the year, Master storyteller, B. Love, is the unparalleled self-love teacher. As the powerhouse for modern-day womanhood, she pens contagious content that encourages readers to internalize admiration and intimacy. She allows her most powerful vessel to guide her stories, wholly. Since age 12, Love has been spreading self-awareness, care, and appreciation. For close to three years, Love has authored over 66 publications centered around heart-piercing, reverence-worthy romance. Her novels not only entertain but challenge the audience to explore love. With a keen eye for passion, desire and dynamism she includes heuristic methods in her beautifully curated accounts of life. B. Love's entire persona is spearheaded by her incredible infatuation with the power of love. Contained within each novel, is an edification created for the glorification of self. Her pen bleeds for the souls who need just an inkling of empowerment. Each story is written with the intent to enlighten, engross and enkindle the passion in whoever picks up her book.

Let's connect!

Made in the USA
Middletown, DE
26 April 2019